Beautiful men were bad news.

Sydney had to remind herself of that as she noted how beautiful Chase was. In a hard, rugged, utterly masculine way.

He turned away from her as his cell phone chirped and the plane began to taxi forward.

Moments later, Chase closed his phone. When he looked at her, the dangerous mercenary had returned full force.

Something, some wild suspicion, an absurdly ridiculous hope, made her ask, "Was that call from Prince Reginald?"

Chase took her hand and leaned forward, compassion turning his hazel eyes dark. "It was the Duke of Carrington, my boss. I'm sorry to have to tell you this, but Prince Reginald, the father of your unborn child, is dead."

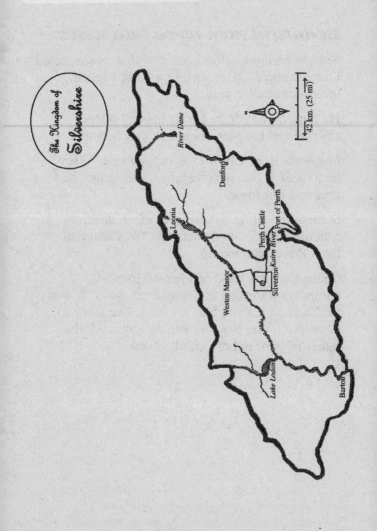

KAREN WHIDDON

THE Princess's SECRET SCANDAL

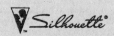

INTIMATE MOMENTS™

Published by Silhouette Books

America's Publisher of Contemporary Romance

Special thanks and acknowledgment are given to
Karen Whiddon for her contribution to the
CAPTURING THE CROWN miniseries.

 SILHOUETTE BOOKS

ISBN 0-373-27486-6

THE PRINCESS'S SECRET SCANDAL

KAREN WHIDDON

started weaving fanciful tales for her younger brothers at the age of eleven. Amidst the Catskill Mountains of New York, then the Rocky Mountains of Colorado, she fueled her imagination with the natural beauty of the rugged peaks and spun stories of love that captivated her family's attention.

Karen now lives in North Texas, where she shares her life with her very own hero of a husband and three doting dogs. Also an entrepreneur, she divides her time between the business she runs with her husband and writing the contemporary romantic suspense and paranormal romances that readers enjoy, and that she now brings to Silhouette Intimate Moments. You can e-mail Karen at KWhiddon1@aol.com or write to her at P.O. Box 820807, Fort Worth, TX 76182. Fans of her writing can also check out her Web site at www.KarenWhiddon.com.

As always, to my lover and best friend,
the man whom I model all the heroes after—
my husband, Lonnie.

Chapter 1

"Are you sure she's—?" Chase Savage broke off, stifling a curse.

A horn honked. Traffic inched slowly forward. He pressed the cell phone against his ear with one hand, keeping the other on the steering wheel while he negotiated the heavy downtown Silverton traffic.

"Yes, of course." His caller chuckled. "Isn't it obvious?"

Though he hated to do so, especially to his boss, as head of the royal publicity department Chase felt he must point out the obvious. "She's avoiding the reporters."

The all-important press. Couldn't live with them, couldn't live without them.

His Grace, Russell Southgate, III, Duke of Carrington, and Chase's employer, made a rude sound. "For now. She's holding out. You know how the game is played. You've dealt with her kind before."

Chase sighed. At the ripe age of twenty-nine, he really *had* seen it all. There seemed to be an endless supply of royal groupies and hangers-on, all wanting something for nothing. Some craved sex, most sought money or a slight slice of fame. Royal fame. Which he knew could often be a royal pain in the ass.

"Are you certain Reginald didn't—" Chase began.

"*His Highness* might be difficult, but he's still next in line for the throne. And this is not just any groupie. Even if she is from the wrong side of the blanket, she's still daughter to Prince Kerwin of Naessa. You know that."

"She doesn't move in the usual circles. I've never met her."

"I know." Carrington sighed again. "Maybe that's what intrigued Reginald. Who knows? Though Reginald is denying everything this time, his mistake could have an enormous impact. Not just Silvershire is affected. The woman says she's pregnant, for God's sake. If this is not handled properly, the situation could become a political disaster." The Duke muttered a particularly un-royal curse, making Chase grin. Unlike most of the royals he spent his time protecting, when Carrington let down his guard, he could be a regular guy. Almost.

"Get to her before she talks to the press. The damage she could do…" Chase could hear the other man shudder, even over the phone line.

"So you want me to 'handle' her?" As a huge, blue SUV cut him off, Chase lay on his horn. "How?"

"With style and class, as usual. Offer her money to take her child and disappear. You can do it, the way only you know how. I have confidence you'll do splendidly, as usual."

The rare compliment, coming from Carrington, told

Chase more than anything how important this was. In the six years since Chase had moved up the ranks from royal bodyguard to publicist, Carrington had been a good employer and a fair boss. He'd been instrumental in Chase's career, taking an interest in the younger man and helping him navigate the sometime intricate maze that comprised royal life.

Effortlessly and tirelessly making the royals look good had earned Chase a promotion to head of public relations. The Wizard of PR, his staff called him. He sort of liked the name.

"I'm on my way to the Hotel Royale now." Chase consulted his watch, a Rolex, which had been an expensive holiday gift Prince Reginald had given half the palace staff. "I should be there in, oh, thirty minutes or less."

Traffic slowed to a stop, forcing Chase to hit his brakes, hard. Rush hour sucked. Most times he managed to avoid the snarl of cars by working late at the palace. Not today. Today he had to hightail it over to the plush hotel in downtown Silverton and intercept this woman before she checked out. Best to confront her in her room, to make the offer in private. Timing was everything in his business.

"You'll handle this." It wasn't a question. Carrington rarely asked. He expected or demanded. And what he wanted, he got.

"Yes, I'll handle it. Never fear." Chase closed his cell phone and turned up the volume on the radio. He'd downloaded and burned a new CD of classic American rock last night. Aerosmith blasted over the speakers, making him grin. Stuck in traffic was as good a time as any to enjoy his favorite tunes.

He saw no need to plot a strategy—groupies were

groupies. Once he started talking money to this woman, he anticipated a quick resolution.

Reaching the hotel, he eschewed the valet parking and drove into the parking garage himself. With the ever-vigilant press always on the lookout for a story, he didn't want to risk being seen.

The Hotel Royale had a back entrance and he used it now. Carrington had given him the woman's room number, so he took the service elevator to the sixth floor. He encountered no one, not even hotel staff. Shifts were changing, and he anticipated another ten or fifteen minutes of privacy.

Moving silently on the plush carpeting, he found her room and shook his head. Her door was ajar, the deadbolt turned out to keep the heavy door from closing. Since maids often did this when cleaning the rooms, he wondered if he'd arrived too late.

Pulling the door open, he saw he was not. With her back to him, a slender woman with shoulder-length, cinnamon-colored hair was loading clothes into an open suitcase she'd placed on the bed.

"Not much of a princess," he drawled. "Where's your entourage? Sydney Conner, I presume?"

Her head snapped up. When she met his gaze, he felt an involuntary tightening low in his gut. Damn. She was heart-stoppingly gorgeous. He'd expected that. They all were.

But this woman was no flashy blonde, Prince Reginald's usual type. Her wealth of thick, silky hair framed a delicate, oval face. With her generous mouth, high cheekbones, and dark blue eyes, she had a serene, quiet sort of beauty, not at all what Chase would have expected from one of Prince Reginald's lovers.

Instant desire—fierce, intense, savage—made him draw a harsh, ragged breath.

Staring at him with wide eyes, she reached for the phone. Calling hotel security, no doubt.

"Wait." He held up his ID. "I'm with the palace."

Her full lips thinned. "Let me see."

He tossed it, surprised when she caught the laminated badge with one elegant, perfectly manicured hand. After she ascertained he really was whom he'd said he was, she replaced the phone in the cradle and narrowed her amazing eyes.

"I locked my door. How did you get in here?"

He gave her a slow smile, his PR smile. "Actually, your door was open. Rather careless, don't you think?"

That caught her off guard. Glancing at the door, she blinked, then frowned. "What can I do for you, Mr...." She studied the badge again, her lush lips curving in a rueful smile. "Savage? I'm on my way out, so this will have to be quick."

Again when she looked at him, he felt that punch to the gut. This time, a flare of anger lanced through his lust.

She was good, he admitted grudgingly. Her every movement was elegant, sensual. Her appearance, from the cut of her expensive, designer clothing to the pampered, creamy glow of her skin, spoke of wealth and breeding. Not your usual palace hanger-on at all.

But then, she *was* a princess.

"Where are you going?"

"That's none of your business," she told him, matching his cool tone. "Since I have little to do with the royal family of Silvershire these days, I don't understand why you're here. What do you want?"

He flashed her a hard look, belatedly remembering at the last moment to soften it with another smile. "As you saw from my ID, I'm with the royal publicity department. His Grace, the Duke of Carrington, sent me."

She stared, her emotions flashing across her mobile face, hope, disbelief and a tentative joy chief among them. She read the badge one last time before handing it back to him.

"Reginald spoke to the duke?" she asked. "He told him about our baby?"

Hearing the raw emotion in her voice, Chase felt a flash of pity. The look she gave him told him she'd seen and hated both that and the fact she'd let her guard down enough to show her feelings to a total stranger.

Chase narrowed his eyes. "I wasn't informed how Lord Carrington learned of your claim."

"But Reginald—" She bit her lip.

"Reginald what?"

One hand instinctively went to her belly. *Protective.* He noted this and filed it away for future reference. "What do you and/or Lord Carrington want with me?"

She was sleek and beautiful and sexy as hell. Chase could think of a thousand ways to answer that question, though he'd say none of them. He had a job to do.

He lifted his briefcase. "I've been authorized to offer you—"

The window exploded in a shower of glass.

"Get down!" He leapt at her.

Too stunned to react when he pushed her down, Sydney fell heavily, the man on top of her. Panicked, terrified the fall had hurt her unborn child, she fought to get up.

"Stay down," he snarled. "That was a gunshot."

"A gunshot? Why would someone shoot at me?"

When he looked at her, she saw a different man. Gone was the affable, smiling stranger. This man wore a grim face, a hard face, the kind of face she'd seen on her mother's bodyguards, hired mercenaries for the most part. Dangerous men who played by their own set of rules.

"Who are you, really?" She whispered, still cradling her abdomen. "You might be in public relations now, but I'm thinking you might have another job title, as well."

He looked away, climbing off her, still keeping low to the ground.

Another shot rang out, taking out what was left of the window.

He cursed. "That window—what's it face?"

Confused, she shook her head. "I'm not sure. I'm on the sixth floor. No view. All that's out there is the roof of one of the lower buildings." Then she realized what that meant. If she were to climb out her window, she'd be able to step without much discomfort onto the other roof.

The shooter was that close! She had to protect her baby.

"We've got to get out of here." He grabbed her hand, yanking her to her feet. "Stay low and follow me."

He started for the door.

She grabbed her purse. "I need my passport."

"Come on." Once they reached the hall, he turned left.

"The elevator's that way." She pointed right.

"We're taking the stairs. Hurry."

They hustled all the way down. Their footsteps clattered on the metal edges, echoing in the narrow stairway.

"Let's go, through here." Tone low and urgent, he shepherded her out a door marked as an emergency exit, instantly setting off the hotel alarm. "Good, a distraction," he shouted over the clanging bell and whirring siren.

Outside, momentarily disoriented, Sydney stumbled, squinting into the bright sunlight. He gave her arm another tug, urging her on, past the line of parked cars on the curb.

"My cello." She suddenly remembered her beloved instrument. "I can't leave it. Go back and get it, please?"

"No. I'll buy you another."

"You don't understand. It's a Stradivarius, one of only sixty left in the world." She attempted in vain to pull herself free, knowing she personally couldn't go back after it. She had to protect her baby at all costs, even if that meant she lost Lady Swister, her cello. "Please," she repeated. "It will only take a moment."

Grim-faced, he stared, sending a chill of foreboding up her spine. "You want me to risk my life for an instrument?"

"A three-million-dollar instrument. Please." She gestured again. "We've obviously lost the shooter."

"For now." A muscle worked in his jaw. "How the hell did you get a three-million-dollar cello?"

"Reginald gave it to me. I—"

They both heard the sharp report of another shot. Seemingly at the same time, the side window of the car behind them shattered.

"Go. Now!" Not hesitating, he yanked her after him.

They took off at a run, across the deserted street and into a narrow alley.

"But my cello…!"

"Forget the cello. This way."

"My rental car's closer." She pointed at the cute red Gaston Mini, parked near the corner. "Right there." Fishing the remote out of her purse, she punched the unlock button.

A second later, the car exploded.

The force of the blast knocked them both to the ground.

An instant and then Chase yanked her to her feet. Dazed, she could only stare at the roaring inferno that, seconds before, had been her car.

"Are you all right?"

She blinked, looked down at her torn slacks and bloody knees. "I…I think so."

Sirens drowned out even the still-clanging hotel alarm. Any minute now, police, ambulance and fire trucks should careen around the corner.

"Good." He tugged at her arm. "Come on then. Run!"

Another gunshot, uncomfortably close, took out another windshield.

"Come on."

They took off running. Several glances over her shoulder and she still couldn't see the gunman, or anyone in pursuit.

Still, she had to protect her baby.

"Don't look back. Just run!" He led her left, then right and left again into a concrete parking garage. Their footsteps echoed as they ran toward a low-slung, black Mercedes.

By the time he bundled her into the car, she was out of breath and panting. Another quick look assured her they hadn't been followed. "So far so good."

"They found your room and anticipated the door we'd exit," he muttered. "It's only a matter of time until they find us. We're not waiting around until they do."

Starting the engine without sparing her a second glance, he shoved the gearshift into reverse, backing so fast his tires squealed. Then he gunned the car forward. The powerful motor roared as they shot into the street. They careened around the corner, barreling toward the main thoroughfare.

Suddenly, she felt every cut, every bruise. Worse than

that, her lower back hurt. Alarm flared through her. Had she injured her baby? Sydney cradled her abdomen, trying to regain her breath, her mind whirling.

"What?" Now he looked at her, his hazel eyes missing nothing. "Are you hurt?"

"No. Yes. I—I don't know." She bit her lip, both hands covering her still-flat abdomen. "I'm pregnant. I'm worried about my baby."

"You don't look pregnant." One hand on the steering wheel, he issued this observation in a bland, bored tone, as if he dealt every day with shootouts and chases. For all she knew, maybe he did.

"I'm barely eight weeks." Stiffening, she refused to look at him again, glancing out the window as she finally took notice of her surroundings. They were heading away from downtown, toward the Silvershire International Airport. "Look, Mr. Savage…"

"Call me Chase."

She ignored him. "Mr. Savage. Where are we going?"

Instead of answering, he gave her another hard look. "Any idea who was shooting at you? And why?"

"No. I think it's more likely we got caught in the middle of someone else's troubles."

"Troubles?"

She waved her hand. "You know. Gang war or something. We were in the wrong place at the wrong time."

"Princess—"

"My name is Sydney."

"Sydney, then. They shot at you. No one else. You. Your car exploded. Of course this was aimed at you."

Lifting her chin, she considered his words. He was right. "Why? Why would anyone want to harm me?"

Keeping an eye on the rearview mirror, he took the exit that led to the airport. "You claim to be carrying the crown prince's child. You know there's a political firestorm going on now with those democracy advocates. That'd put you right in the middle of it."

"True. But Reginald and I aren't married. My baby is no threat to anyone."

"Yet," he said.

"Ever." Closing her mouth before she said too much more, Sydney caught sight of the Welcome to Silvershire International Airport sign. "Where are you taking me? Why the airport?"

For the first time since appearing in her doorway, he looked surprised. As though she should have known. "The royal jet is waiting."

"The royal jet?" A tentative spark of hope filled her. "Has he asked you to bring me to him?"

"Who?"

Impatient, she shifted in her seat. "Reginald, of course. My baby's father. Are you taking me to see him?"

There was no pity in the hard glance he shot her now.

"No," he said. Nothing more.

But then, what else could he say? Reginald had made it plain he didn't want her or the unplanned baby she carried. She'd even learned he'd gotten engaged to a beautiful princess from Gastonia. He'd moved quickly, proving his words of love had been nothing but lies.

The knowledge shouldn't hurt so much, but it did. Mostly, she thought with a wry smile, because she'd unintentionally done the one thing she'd always sworn not to. She'd inadvertently mimicked her mother's life.

When she looked up she realized Chase watched her and

most likely had misinterpreted her smile. No matter, she was going home to Naessa soon. Then what he or anyone else in the country of Silvershire thought wouldn't matter a whit. Not at all.

She'd managed to do as her mother had done, but unlike her mother, she wouldn't ever call her baby a mistake. From now on, Sydney had a child to think of. From now on, her baby would always come first.

A quick glance at the handsome man beside her told her nothing. Chase Savage had protected her, but what were his real intentions?

They pulled up to an iron gate marked Private. Chase pushed a button on his console and the barricade swung open. Driving slowly through the rows of hangars, he punched in a number on his cell phone, a razor-thin model which looked like something out of a James Bond movie. He spoke a few terse words—not enough for her to glean the gist of the conversation, and snapped the metal phone closed.

"All settled," he said cheerfully. "I've gotten us emergency clearance." They turned right, into the airport's private section. Sydney had flown out of here before, as most of her friends' families were wealthy. Here, in various hangars, the rich kept their personal jets. No doubt the royal family had several.

"Emergency clearance for what?" she asked, as they pulled up in front of a nondescript, gray metal hangar. "If Reginald—" she swallowed tightly as she spoke the name "—didn't send for me, then why'd you bring me here at all?"

He frowned. "I had to take you somewhere safe."

"Not really." Studying him, she wished she could read his closed expression. "I'm not your responsibility. As a matter of fact, why are you—head of Silvershire's public relations department—here to begin with?"

For the first time since he'd appeared in her hotel room, cool, confident Chase Savage appeared at a loss for words.

She pressed her advantage. "You started to say something earlier, before the shooting started. You said you'd been authorized to do something. What was it?"

"Not now." He shook his head. "We'll discuss that later, once we're in the air."

"In the air to…?"

"I'm taking you home, to Naessa. You'll be safer there than here."

"Home?" Exactly where she wanted to go. Except… "I need my cello." The Strad could never be replaced.

"I'll send someone after your instrument," he promised. "The police should be there by now. They won't let anyone mess with it."

"I need to see a doctor and make sure everything is all right with the baby."

"You can do that once you get home. It's only a forty-five-minute flight to Naessa."

Something still bothered her, though she wasn't sure what. He'd addressed her every concern smoothly. Too smoothly. Maybe that was the problem.

She glanced around them. "This doesn't look like the royal hangar. Where's the Silvershire crest?"

Expression implacable, he shrugged. "The king won't allow that because of the danger from terrorists. The royal crest could act as a huge bull's-eye for undesirables."

He had a point, though she hated the word he'd used. *Undesirables.* In Naessa, as the king's unacknowledged daughter, she'd been called that and a lot worse. *Bastard* had been her mother's particular favorite. For a while Frances had adopted it almost as a nickname, referring to Sydney as her bastard spawn, reminding her at an early age how she'd ruined her mother's life.

Sydney vowed her child—son or daughter, whichever— would only enrich hers.

Chase got out of the car and crossed around the front to Sydney's side, opening her door and holding out his hand. She slipped her hand into his larger one, noting the calluses on his long, elegant fingers, and allowed him to help her from the low-slung car.

Staring up at his rugged face, Sydney wondered about his ancestry. Though he wore a well-cut, conservative suit, his shaggy hair and hawklike features made him appear dangerous. She wouldn't be surprised to learn he had a trace of pirate in him.

As if he'd read her thoughts, he smiled, stunning her. He really was, she noted abstractly, struggling to find her breath, quite beautiful. In a hard, rugged, utterly masculine way.

She reminded herself that beautiful men were bad news. Reginald had provided her with living proof of that.

Once Chase had closed the door behind her with a quiet thunk, she had another round of misgivings and tugged her hand free. While private jet was always more comfortable than commercial, she barely knew this man.

"We don't have time for this." He consulted his Rolex, shooting her a look of pure male exasperation.

The watch looked familiar. Ah, yes. Reginald had gifted all his staff with similar watches for Christmas.

"Shall we go?"

Finally she nodded.

Up the steps into the waiting jet they went. A short,

blond man greeted them. Evidently, he was one of the pilots. He pulled the door closed before disappearing into the cockpit.

Sydney had time to note the jet's plush interior before one side of the hangar opened like a giant, automatic garage door.

Chase barely glanced at her. "Buckle your seat belt."

His cell phone chirped. Immediately, he answered, turning away from her to try and conduct his business with a measure of privacy.

The plane began to taxi forward.

Chase closed his phone and then powered off. When he looked at her, the dangerous mercenary had returned, full-force.

"What is it?" she asked. Something, some wild suspicion, an absurdly ridiculous hope, made her ask. "Was that call from Reginald?"

His hazel gaze touched on her coolly. "Is that why you came to Silvershire? To see the prince?"

"Of course. I wanted him to look me in the face and tell me…"

"Tell you what?"

"Never mind." No way was she admitting to this man, this stranger, the depth of her shame. Reginald had pretended to love her. And now, when she carried his child, a baby they'd made together, he pretended he didn't know her. She sighed. "Forget I asked that. It was foolish of me."

Chase watched her a heartbeat longer, then he dipped his head, his hazel eyes shuttered.

Another thought occurred to her. "Is this plan to remove me from your country carried out at Reginald's direction?"

"No." He gave her a long, hard look. "This is entirely

spur-of-the-moment. Not planned. After what happened back at the hotel, I had no choice. It's not safe for you in Silvershire. Especially now."

That caught her attention. "Especially now?"

"That phone call…Things have changed," Chase said softly, as though his words could hurt her.

"Why? What's happened?" She searched his hard, rugged face. "What are you not telling me?"

He took her hand and leaned forward, compassion turning his hazel eyes dark. "That phone call I just got? It was the Duke of Carrington, my boss. I'm sorry to have to tell you this, but Prince Reginald, the father of your unborn child, is dead."

Chapter 2

"Dead?"

Her amazing eyes widened as she took in his words. Shock and disbelief flashed across her face. *She hadn't known.* Russell had been so certain, but he'd been wrong.

Sydney Conner was hearing the news for the first time. Chase would bet his life on that.

"Dead?" She repeated, bewilderment echoing in her husky voice. "Reginald? Are you sure?"

Still watching her closely, he nodded. Unbelievably, he had a random urge to touch her, to stroke her creamy skin and soothe the grief from her face. Instead, he clenched his jaw and kept his hands to himself.

"When?" Her husky voice vibrated with sadness.

"He died last night, at his country estate. We—that is, the royal public relations department—have a press conference scheduled for—" he glanced at his watch "—right about now."

"A press conference?" She said the words as though they were foreign. Again her sapphire gaze searched his face. "You're telling the truth? Reginald…is…really… dead?"

"Yes." He kept his own face expressionless. "You'll see it in the papers tomorrow."

Though her hands shook, she felt no immediate sense of loss. She'd already lost Reginald the day he'd walked away from her and the child they'd created. He'd made it plain he wanted nothing further to do with the woman he'd once courted so ardently.

The foolish woman, a bitter smile curved her lips, *who'd trusted his words of love.* "I can't believe it."

He said nothing, merely continuing to hold her hand and watch her.

Reginald. Dead. Now her baby would never have a chance to know its father. Even though Reginald had refused to acknowledge her pregnancy, she'd had hopes he would change once the child was born.

Even though her own sire hadn't.

"Was there an accident? How…how did he die?"

"No accident. There's some speculation it was a drug overdose. Other than that, I don't know. They haven't begun the autopsy. I'm sure I'll be notified—as will the press—when they know anything."

"Overdose?"

"You didn't know he did drugs?"

Slowly, she shook her head. Pulling her hand free, she pressed herself into the seat. Tension began to build in her shoulders. For an instant, she longed for Camille, her talented, personal masseuse back home in Naessa, and she rubbed her aching neck. The beginnings of a headache started behind her eyes. Damn it. She felt vaguely guilty, though she knew her wishing him dead had nothing to do with what had actually happened.

Though he'd dumped her and scorned their child, Reginald didn't deserve to die.

"Are you all right?"

She'd been so lost in her own thoughts she'd managed almost to forget he was there. *Almost* being the key word. She doubted people often forgot a man like Chase Savage. Even sitting still, he dominated the cabin space.

"I'm fine," she murmured. "I think."

For a moment she thought she saw compassion in his hazel eyes. Because she didn't want that, she swallowed and lifted her chin. "Did you know Reginald well?"

"*Prince* Reginald?" He raised his brows. "He was a bit out of my stratosphere."

What could she say to that? "He was out of everyone's stratosphere."

"What about you?" he asked. "How'd you meet him?"

"After a performance." A thousand bittersweet memories rushed back to her. He'd sent her flowers the first night. And every night after that, in every city in which the symphony had performed. He'd come backstage every single time, charming her fellow performers, his dark and hooded gaze focused on her. Only on her.

Afraid, she'd refused his invitation to dinner. Again and again. Her refusals never seemed to faze him, for he'd continued to ask until finally, wearily, she gave in. After all, as he'd pointed out, it was merely a simple meal. What objections could she have to eating?

That dinner had been the beginning of her downfall.

"Reliving the excitement?" Though his tone was kind, he gave her a mocking smile.

Without thinking, she shook her head. "Just remembering," she told him softly. "Reginald was a charismatic man." She wouldn't tell him the rest. "His death will be felt by many."

"Perhaps." Chase gave her an odd look. "But then, of course, you must have seen a different side of him."

Before Reginald's betrayal, Sydney could have talked about him for hours, and cherished every word. She'd believed he'd loved her, she who'd been so patently unloved her entire life. She'd bloomed under his attention. Now that she knew the truth, that she'd merely been a flavor of the month to him, she felt foolish. What she'd mistaken for love on her own part was mere infatuation. But she'd refused to retreat into her safe little shell. For her baby's sake, she'd pursued Reginald back to his own country, determined to give her child what she herself had never had. A father.

Staring blindly out her window, she realized the light-colored fog had changed, darkened.

She took a deep breath. "You still haven't told me why you're here. In view of what's happened, I think I should know."

After a moment, he nodded. "As you know, I'm head of public relations for Silvershire. Prince Reginald forwarded the e-mails you sent him to the duke, who dispatched me to handle you."

"Handle me?" As though she was some royal hanger-on who now presented a problem.

"Yes. I was sent to check you out." His gaze swept over her, making her insides tighten.

"Now it no longer matters. Reginald is dead. My baby will never know its father now."

"No longer matters?" He watched her closely. "You aren't going to try and claim rights to the throne?"

After a startled moment, she could only shake her head. "I have no reason to do that. If King Weston wants my child to be named heir, then I would consider it."

"Your child has royal blood. Not just Reginald's but yours. You're Prince Kerwin's daughter."

"Bastard daughter." She smiled, a pro at hiding the hurt. "There's a world of difference between the two. Believe me. That's why I find it difficult to believe that someone wants to kill me. I'm important to no one, especially my sire."

Hearing her own words, she winced. She hadn't meant to reveal so much to this employee of Silvershire's royal family.

"I still think the attack was because you're carrying Reginald's baby."

"Why would that matter? Reginald and I were not married. My child," she swallowed, forcing herself to say the hateful words, "is illegitimate." Like her. "A bastard child can never be heir. Believe me, I should know that better than anyone."

"True, but the playing field has changed. The prince is dead. Your child is the last of the royal bloodline."

"I care little about that. Being a princess has only brought me discomfort and unwanted attention."

"Unwanted?" He still watched her closely. "Is that why you haven't gone to the newspapers or granted a television interview?"

He sounded incredulous, but then he was in public relations. Nothing would be more important to him than the press.

She couldn't tell him she didn't want to be like her own mother, who seemed to spend much of her life courting reporters, while Sydney had been, until Reginald, able to skirt the edges of their radar. She'd like to return to her former quiet life, if possible. "I'd prefer to avoid notoriety."

His incredulous expression told her he didn't believe her. "You're saying you'd actually shun the limelight? You're an illegitimate princess who's been largely overlooked. Until now. I know how this works. You'll bask in your fifteen minutes of fame, just like anyone else."

Like any other groupie, he meant. As her mother had been. Still was, as far as she knew. Sydney no longer spoke to her mother. "I repeat, I'd prefer a quiet life."

"You could make a lot of money exploiting this."

"I have plenty of money," she said stiffly. "My sire set up a trust fund for me. And, as I'm sure you know, I play cello with the Naessa Royal Symphony."

"True, but now you'll have a child to support. One can always use more money."

She looked out the window instead of attempting to dignify his comments with a response. They'd flown into dark clouds. Lightning flashed to the west, and rain splattered the jet's windows.

Inhaling, exhaling, she willed herself calm. Years of yoga, breathing exercises and even hypnosis had helped conquer her unreasonable terror of storms.

The jet banked sharply to the right.

An involuntary gasp escaped her.

Chase smiled reassuringly. "Don't worry. I think it's just

one of those sudden spring thunderstorms. If it had been forecast, we wouldn't have flown anywhere near it. I'm sure we'll go around. Franco's flown this jet a hundred times or more, and Dell's been his copilot for years."

Before he finished speaking, the jet dropped, a rapid bounce, pushing Sydney up and against the confines of her seat belt before she bounced back. "What the—?"

"Turbulence."

Since Chase's implacable face showed no signs of alarm, Sydney took his words at face value. His very serenity was soothing, though she found herself wondering if the man was ever alarmed at anything.

The rain began to pound them. Thunder boomed. Lightning flashed stronger and more often. It looked as though they'd flown right into the middle of the worst part of the storm.

"I thought you said he'd take us around?"

"I'm sure he's trying. We're climbing, can't you feel it? This must be a large storm, so he's probably trying to get above it instead of going around."

All logical and competent-sounding. Still, Sydney's gut instinct was sounding multiple alarms. Her absolute fear of storms came roaring back, intensified by the fact she was being tossed around in a small jet.

She took a deep, shaky breath. "It's green outside."

For the first time, Chase frowned. "That's not good."

Her stomach plummeted. Was that the understatement of the year? She gripped her seat, closed her eyes, and muttered a prayer. When she opened her eyes, she immediately looked to Chase. He watched her intently.

"You're absolutely terrified." He sounded surprised.

Wordless with fear, she jerked her head in a nod.

"It's going to be all right. Look." He pointed out the window. "We're still climbing. Soon we should be above the storm."

Even as he spoke, the first hail hit them. Small, round balls of ice began battering the wings. Next came what sounded like a series of pops in rapid succession. Outside, the ice balls grew larger, more numerous, pummeling the wings. The jet veered left, then right.

"We've got to give Franco and Dell credit." Admiration sounded in Chase's clear tone. "They're still climbing."

The air outside her window became all ice balls, so many it appeared to be a blizzard of ice.

Bam. Sydney jumped, gripping the sides of her seat so tightly her hands ached. "That sounded like a small explosion." She'd barely finished the words when the jet plummeted again. Muttering another quick prayer under her breath, she bit her lip to stifle a scream, unable to resist glancing at Chase for reassurance.

Though expressionless, the tight set of his jaw told her he was worried, too.

The dive lasted longer this time. It seemed, she thought, fighting the first edges of panic, to go on forever.

Were they about to crash into the ocean? Or worse, into the mountainous edge of Silvershire? She had no idea where they were or what might be below them.

Then again, if they crashed at this speed, what they hit wouldn't really matter.

Finally the plane leveled.

Sydney exhaled in relief.

"Despite his attempt to climb, I think we've lost a lot of altitude." Chase sounded calm, matter-of-fact, as though none of this worried him. "I'd better go talk to Franco." He pushed himself out of his seat and the plane lurched, then took another violent drop.

He lost his balance and stumbled toward Sydney.

Wide-eyed, she reacted instinctively, throwing up her arms. He stopped with his face inches from her breasts.

God help her, she could feel her face heating.

Slowly, he raised his head to meet her gaze. She could have sworn she saw a flicker of amusement in his hazel eyes before he climbed back to his feet. "My apologies."

Tongue-tied, she dipped her head in acknowledgment.

"Wait here," he ordered, making his way to the cockpit.

As if she planned on going anywhere! She grimaced as the jet pitched and bobbed. If she had a parachute, she'd definitely consider jumping. She flexed her shoulders, feeling tension knots as she stared at the closed cockpit door.

A moment later, Chase returned. His expression looked even grimmer, if such a thing was possible.

She straightened, her aches forgotten. "What? What's wrong?"

"Not good. We've lost an engine. The hail must have damaged it."

Her heart stopped. "What now?"

"Franco and Dell are good. They're searching for a place to make an emergency landing. They'll get us down safely."

"With one engine?"

"Yes. We'll be fine."

Swallowing, she pushed back her panic. She'd traveled a lot with the symphony, and knew this wasn't great, but it wasn't lethal.

Thunder boomed again, so loudly the jet shook. A jagged bolt of lightning flashed so close she wondered how it had missed them. Though the hail had tapered off and was mixed with driving rain, the storm's fury scared her almost as much as the possibility of crashing.

"Talk to me." Not caring that her desperation showed in her voice, she touched his arm. "I need a distraction."

Another man might have made light of her fear. But Chase took one look at her and nodded. "Tell me about your family."

She had no family. "I'd rather hear about yours. Do you have brothers and sisters?"

"I have two brothers and two sisters." He smiled fondly. "We're a noisy, affectionate bunch. They're all married now, and their spouses are part of the family, as well."

"But you've never been married?" Gripping her seat, she wondered why she'd asked, but as the plane did another hop-and-skip movement and she felt her stomach come up in her throat, she realized she didn't care.

"No," he said, his expression closed. For a moment she could have sworn she saw a flash of anger and hurt in his eyes, and she wondered.

Then she remembered. She'd read about him a few years back. Chase might work at keeping the royal family out of the news, but that meant his own life was up for public scrutiny, as well.

"You were engaged," she said slowly. "To the daughter of an earl. I remember now. And there was some sort of scandal, involving another—"

"Yes." His harsh voice cut at her like a knife. "I was engaged. It didn't work out. No need to rehash all the details."

There had been a baby, Sydney remembered. Another man's child, though the woman had tried to pass it off as his to get him to marry her. The wedding ceremony had actually started when the woman's lover, a high-ranking duke from Gastonia, had interrupted, claiming both the woman and the baby as his rather than Chase's. While flashbulbs popped and cameras whirled, Chase had learned the truth. In front of the entire world, he'd been jilted.

The repercussions had nearly cost him his job. Though he'd presented a stone face to any and all questions, and had since cut a wide swath through Silvershire's female population, Sydney knew how badly he must have been hurting.

After all, she could certainly relate.

"Did you love her?" she asked softly.

Instead of answering, he narrowed his eyes. "Did you love Reginald? Did you truly believe he was the one you'd spend the rest of your life loving?"

Throat tight, she nodded.

Emotion flashed in his gaze. Rage or torment, she couldn't tell which. "Then I think we're about equal, aren't we? We both know what it's like to be played for a fool."

As she opened her mouth to apologize, a dark-haired man appeared in the doorway of the cockpit. The copilot, Dell. All the color seemed to have drained from his face.

"Chase." One word, then he went back to his controls.

Instantly, Chase unbuckled and took off for the front of the plane. While he was gone, though the jet seemed steadier, she could have sworn they now descended rather than climbed.

An eternity seemed to pass before he returned.

His expression hard, he stood staring at her for a moment before dropping down into his seat and refastening the seat belt.

"Chase?" She touched his arm. "What did he want?"

"To give me bad news." The gaze that met hers was

bleak. "If you're a praying person, you'd better start now. Though he's bringing us down to try and land, the other engine has sustained damage, too. Franco doesn't know how much longer it will last."

She stared at him, a stranger until that very morning, and twice the bearer of bad news. "We're going to crash?"

A muscle worked in his jaw. "It certainly looks that way."

God help her, she didn't want to die the same way she'd lived her life—alone. But she wasn't alone, she had her baby. Her unborn child.

Once, music had been enough. She'd thought her art was her life, her reason for existence, her sole, all-consuming passion. The weight and solid feel of her cello, the pure, smooth sound of her gleaming horsehair bow gliding across the strings, had been her everything. Until now.

Now her baby mattered more than anything.

She had to live so her child could be born. Grabbing Chase's hand, she gripped his fingers. "I can't believe this. I'm not ready."

He unhooked his seat belt. "Come here."

"What?" She stared blankly. "What do you mean?"

His expression compassionate, he pushed the buckle and freed her from her own restraint. "Come here."

Still she resisted. "But isn't it safer to stay buckled in?"

"Maybe. Maybe not. But there's no way in hell either of us need to go through this alone. Now come here."

He pulled her out of her seat and into his arms.

At first, she held herself stiffly. But the human need for contact and comfort outweighed any other considerations and she relaxed. Chase was bigger than she'd expected, and the lean hardness of his body felt reassuring.

Heart pounding, she let her shoulder rest against his chest. Once she'd settled in, arms around his neck, his around her waist, he refastened his seat belt so they were secured together.

"Okay?" he asked.

She nodded, trying to keep her breathing even, resisting the impulse to gulp air, knowing if she started hyperventilating, she'd pass out. And she didn't want that. If there was a way to save herself and her baby, she needed to stay awake and take it.

The plane bucked and, once again, straightened itself out. Sydney released a breath she hadn't even been aware of holding, and a tremor shook her.

"Steady." His deep voice rumbled from his chest. Under her ear, his heartbeat pounded.

She looked up at him, a stranger, a rugged, beautiful man, and caught herself wishing she'd met him earlier, at another time and place. "I don't want to die."

"Me neither. I'm just hoping Franco and Dell can bring us down safely."

"Isn't there anything else we can do?"

"Yeah." A ghost of a grim smile crossed his face. "Pray."

The plane took another odd skip and it seemed their descent had become a plunge.

Sydney shuddered.

Chase smoothed her hair with his tanned hand. "Take it easy. They've still got it under control."

The lights winked out. The interior of the cabin went black.

Chapter 3

Something burning…smoke. Sydney tossed her head restlessly, sure she was dreaming, but wondering why she hurt so badly.

Experimentally, she moved. And groaned. She ached, she hurt and she felt as if she'd been pummeled senseless by an angry giant with a hard fist.

Her baby! Opening her eyes, she found she was lying on craggy rocks, too close to the gently lapping waves for comfort. Smoke billowed from a cluster of trees nearby, and she smelled the acrid scent of aviation gas.

Jet fuel.

She was soaked, as though she'd been in the water and somehow made her way to the shore. Since she had no conscious memory of doing so, she was lucky she hadn't drowned.

Lifting her head, she winced as pain lanced through

her. She touched her aching shoulder. Her hand came away sticky with blood. Blinking, she stared at her red fingers, and bit back a sob. What on earth…?

A piece of metal looked as though it had been stabbed into the ground nearby.

The plane crash!

Though it hurt, she turned her head again, toward the smoke, looking for Chase. Was he there, near the fire?

"Chase?" She tried to yell, but her voice would only croak. She had to get up, get over there, and see if she could help rescue him or Franco and Dell.

Swallowing, wincing as even that small movement hurt, Sydney told herself she had to get up, move away from the ever-encroaching waves and find Chase.

She couldn't make her body move. She lifted her head, trying to see the rest of her, to ascertain whether she'd been injured worse than she knew. Apart from her aching head and stiff neck, and the now-throbbing cut on her side, she felt no other actual pains.

Then why couldn't she push herself to her feet?

A small explosion rocked the beach. More smoke billowed out from behind the row of trees. The jet, most likely. She should be glad she'd been thrown farther away.

Thrown. All at once, the staggering truth of what had happened hit her. Miraculously, she'd survived a plane crash.

So far.

She refused to think anything negative. She was alive. That counted for a lot. From the looks of things, it appeared she might be the only one who had survived. She and the tiny, precious life growing inside her. She could only pray her unborn child was all right. At least she had no cuts on her abdomen, no aches or bloodstains to indicate she'd mis-carried.

Her baby *had* to be all right. More than anything, she prayed her unborn child had not been injured.

She finally struggled to her feet. Standing, weaving, she licked her lip and tasted blood and salt and sweat. Thirsty, so thirsty. She swayed, her vision blurry, and then forced herself to focus. Focus. Live.

A blur moved toward her, moving fast in the blinding sunlight. An animal? No, a man. Running toward her. Shielding her eyes against the sun, she squinted as she tried to make him out.

Chase? Her heart rate tripled. Could it be? She rubbed her blurry eyes and again attempted to focus. Yes, Chase. Moving toward her. Whole. Unhurt.

Glancing down at herself, she winced at her bloody, torn blouse. She swayed again, dropping to her knees. Damn, her head hurt. She might be injured there, too.

"Sydney!" Chase. Blinking, she lifted her head and attempted a feeble wave.

He ran toward her. His lips moved, but she couldn't understand his words. She stared at him, resisting the urge to reach out her hand and sob in relief. He'd made it through the crash in even better shape than she. Except for a still-bleeding, jagged cut on his leg, he appeared to be unhurt.

Good. Then maybe he could help her, until rescue arrived.

Her last conscious memory was of Chase scooping her up in his strong arms.

When the plane went down, damned if Chase's first thought wasn't for the woman. Maybe it was the part of him that would always be a bodyguard, but he'd known he needed to shelter her, protect her and keep her safe, even if it took his own life to do so.

Then everything went black as they'd hit.

When he'd come to in the midst of the smoking wreckage, smelling jet fuel and feeling the searing heat of the fire, Sydney was nowhere to be found. He'd known he had to get out of there before the whole thing blew, but first, he'd looked for the others.

Franco and Dell were dead. After swiftly ascertaining there was no hope for them, Chase knew he didn't have time to drag their bodies from the smoldering wreckage. He needed to get out quickly, aware an explosion was imminent.

He saw no sign of Sydney.

He crawled from the battered jet and, after looking around once more, Chase took off at a run. He made it a hundred yards before the thing exploded, knocking him to the sand.

On all fours, he said a quick prayer for the two dead men. Then he stood and brushed dirt and gravel from his legs. Most of his cuts and scratches appeared to be minor. One wound on his knee bled but he felt no pain.

He began by searching the immediate area around the wreckage. They'd come down in a hilly area, clipping the tops of the massive trees before crashing near the rocky beach.

Sydney—or her body—had to be here somewhere. They'd been strapped in together. How they'd been separated in the final moments, he couldn't begin to speculate.

She wasn't anywhere near the wreckage. Next, he expanded the search area, more and more worried when he still couldn't locate her. The forest area was thick and wild;

still he searched through the dense foliage with no luck. While searching, he came across a spring-fed pond and noted its location. A source of drinkable water would be vital to their survival if they weren't rescued quickly.

As he ranged the perimeter of the woods, pushing aside thorns and vines and undergrowth, he drew closer and closer to the rocky shoreline. As he began to scan the rocks near the water, he heard a hoarse cry up the beach.

There—past the larger boulders, too close to the gently pounding surf, Sydney! When she attempted to rise and sank back down to all fours, his heart stuttered.

"I'm coming!" he yelled, taking off at a run toward the ocean. When he reached her, she tried again to stand.

Bleeding from her wounds and weak, she fainted in his arms.

But she was alive. That was all that mattered.

Carrying her back to the shade of the forest, he lowered her gently to a pile of leaves. Lifting her torn blouse, he ran his hands over her, searching for broken bones and finding none. If she had internal injuries, that would be another matter and much more difficult to detect.

She moaned, shifting fitfully. She had a nasty cut on her shoulder, another on the back of her head, though it looked worse than it was due to the way head wounds bled.

If she had a concussion, which seemed highly likely, he couldn't let her remain unconscious.

"Sydney, wake up."

No response.

Chase heaved a sigh and lifted her to her feet. Her deep-blue eyes opened, cloudy with confusion.

"Come on, we've got to walk." Still bearing the brunt of her weight, he half dragged, half carried her into the forest, toward the pond he'd found earlier. If he could get Sydney there, they could wash off the blood, making it easier to judge the true extent of her wounds.

"Walk?" She shook her head, trying to drop back to the ground. She would have succeeded, but he kept his arm around her waist. "No. I want to sleep."

"No can do." He let her lean on him while they pressed through the undergrowth, and he did a rapid assessment of the situation.

Plane down, two survivors. No working radio; at least, the one in the jet had blown with it. His cell phone had disappeared in the crash—with his luck it had fallen into the ocean. And, though they'd filed a flight plan when they'd left Silvershire, he didn't know if the storm had taken them off course or how far.

They were on some sort of island. Though small, it appeared hospitable. The place was most likely some rich bastard's private getaway, though the area where the plane had gone down didn't appear cultivated. Chase resolved to explore it later, especially if rescue took some time.

All their hope would be on the jet's emergency beacon. Even if it had been damaged or destroyed in the fire, a signal should have already gone out to lead rescuers to them.

Or the bad guys, assuming they had someone on the inside.

They had to be extremely careful.

Chase cursed again. He felt as though he was once again in Special Forces, on some kind of covert mission, rather than the head of Silvershire's Department of Public Relations. More than anything, he wanted a working cell phone. He needed to get in touch with the office and fill them in.

He could only imagine the public relations nightmare going on back home. Since Reginald had died, he'd bet things had gone to hell in a handbasket. With so much going on, Chase needed to be back in Silvershire *now.*

He lived for his work. Except for the brief derailment when he'd thought he'd fallen in love with Kayla Bright, he'd focused his entire life on his job. Always had, always would.

Now, stranded on an island with the one woman the press would be salivating over, he'd been rendered virtually useless. Public relations was difficult to manage when one had no contact with the public.

As he thought of the press, circling like sharks in search of a meal, he realized he'd now become a potential story. Once the reporters realized he and the beautiful woman who carried the prince's son were lost together, they'd be fabricating the stories as fast as the papers could print them.

Christ. Carrington would be furious; he might even feel betrayed. After what had happened with Kayla… Chase shuddered. He'd thought he'd loved her enough to ask her to become his wife. When she'd tricked him into believing another man's baby was his and then jilted him publicly, his own personal anguish had been splashed all over the papers. His infatuation with Kayla had nearly cost him his job once. Only Carrington's interference had saved him and his tattered reputation.

Never again.

This situation had too many common denominators.

Such publicity, even if unwarranted, was exactly the kind of derailment Chase's career didn't need.

He shook his head. Silvershire—and his job—seemed thousands of miles away. Now, stuck for God knows how long on this deserted island, staying alive took precedence over anything else.

Sydney stumbled and nearly fell. The wound on her neck had started bleeding again. Her expensive outfit, torn and dirty and bloodstained, was ruined. Since she had nothing else to wear, all he could do was see what parts of it were salvageable. Either that, or else she'd have to run around using leaves to cover herself, like Eve outside the Garden of Eden. A sudden mental image of Sydney, her sleek curves glistening in the sunlight, nearly had him staggering.

Luckily, he was able to regain his balance.

Finally, they reached the pond. At the edge of the water, he stopped. Sydney looked up at him, her dazed expression telling him she might be going into shock.

"Are you all right?" he asked, his tone gentle.

She licked her lips and tried twice before finally answering. "I think so."

"We're going to get into the water here and get cleaned up. I'll hold on to you, I promise." He took the first step forward, pleased when she moved with him.

The first step took them in up to her waist.

She gasped and began shivering. "Cold!"

"Not really." He knew he had to hurry, because victims of shock had to be kept warm. "Hold still and let me clean you off."

Teeth chattering, she did as he asked. He told himself as he swept his hands over her wet skin, that his touch was impersonal. Nevertheless, his hands on the curve of her hips, her flat belly, felt as if they were touching forbidden fruit. When he accidentally brushed her full breasts and felt her nipples hard against his palm, his body responded, despite the cool water temperature.

He concentrated on cleaning her up and ignored his libido's bad timing.

"I need you to put your head under the water," he said. "Do you want me to dunk you or can you do it yourself?"

Though she still shivered violently, when she looked at him he saw her gaze had cleared. "I can do it, if you hold on to me."

At his nod, she gulped air and dropped under. When she resurfaced, slicking her hair back from her face, his breath caught in his throat. Damned if she didn't look like some primitive nymph, sleek skin gleaming in the dappled sunlight. The shreds of her wet clothing clung to her body and outlined every hollow, every curve.

He was so hard he hurt.

Self-directed anger made him gruff. "Good enough." Helping her up onto the bank, he tried to ignore the way his hand cupped her rounded bottom. Once he was certain she'd be okay, he dived under himself, swimming with powerful strokes to the middle of the pond. Here, he trod water, reminding himself to come back later and explore the depth.

As soon as he had his body under control again, he emerged. Sydney sat, huddled into a wet ball, shivering.

"Let's get you back into the sunlight to warm you."

Docilely, she allowed him to lead her back to the beach area, where he sat her on a huge boulder in full sun.

Now, he needed to see what he could do to make them shelter.

A large side section of the jet had landed on the rocky beach. It would make a decent roof, much better than any primitive thatch thing he might attempt to construct from leaves and sticks.

He grabbed the section of metal and started dragging it toward the trees. It was heavier than he'd realized.

As he moved it inch by inch, dragging it over rocky ground, he wondered how long they'd have to wait until rescue arrived. He refused to consider the possibility that someone else might get here first.

Sydney opened her eyes to find Chase watching her closely, his hazel gaze unreadable. She licked her lips and he handed her a tin cup of water. "The cup is left from what remains of the jet's galley. I found several of them—and a spring-fed pond—near the interior of this island."

She sipped gratefully, her throat still raw. "My baby…"

He looked away, obviously ill at ease. Instead of answering a question that could not be answered, he tried to distract her. "I found your purse, too." He held up the black Fendi. "Remarkably intact. Not even a scratch."

Throat aching, chest tight, she nodded. She really didn't care about the purse, other than being glad to have her passport. She had more important matters to think about. Until she could get to a hospital, she had no idea if her baby was all right. "How long have I been out?"

"You drifted in and out all of last night. I've been keeping watch. When you finally fell into a real sleep, I slept some. Now it's morning." Again he glanced at his wrist, then gave a wry smile. "Though I don't know the exact time. Your watch is gone, too."

"That's okay." She sat up, waiting for dizziness and felt absurdly pleased when the earth didn't spin. They were in some kind of small shelter, made of bits and pieces of the crashed jet. He'd piled sticks and branches near one side, no doubt for when they needed to build a fire. "Where are the pilots?"

"They're both dead. When the cockpit exploded, they

burned." A shadow crossed Chase's rugged face. He had a good five-o'clock-shadow going, which had the effect of making him look even more dangerously masculine. He was so beautiful, looking at him made her chest hurt.

Sydney shook her head. She'd survived a plane crash, minor injuries, and felt like her insides had been scrambled. Had the bump on her head permanently addled her wits? She focused instead on his words, remembering the blond man who'd flown the jet. "I'm sorry."

Chase looked away. "I wanted to bury them, but I couldn't get them out in time." His low voice was tight, controlled, but she thought she could detect an undercurrent of grief.

Wincing, she nodded. "How long before someone comes for us?"

Chase raised his head and met her gaze again. "I don't know. The jet's radio was broken. My cell phone's gone. I have no way to contact anyone. All I can hope is the plane's emergency beacon did its job."

Still woozy, she pushed to her feet, waving him away when he tried to steady her. "We can stand up in here." The shelter he'd improvised for them was nothing short of amazing. He'd anchored pieces of metal from the jet between three trees, using the middle one as a brace. It looked, she thought, quite sturdy, considering.

He saw her looking and shrugged. "It'll do until we're rescued."

She seized on his words, allowing them to give her hope. "I'm sure it will," she told him. "Provided rescue comes soon."

She stepped out from under the shelter to brilliant sunshine. Shading her eyes with her hand, she glanced toward the beach, noting the way the sun reflected off the sea. "So we have water, but what about food? Would it be too much to hope some food survived the crash?"

"A few packets of crackers. That's it. But I've seen some small game in the woods. And of course, there are fish."

"Can you hunt?"

He gave her a supremely male look of arrogance. "Of course I can hunt. I fish, too. We won't starve, if it comes to that." He coughed. "But my cooking is abysmal."

"Cooking's no problem. I can cook." Pushing her hair back from her face, she busied herself organizing the wood in a neat stack. "That is, if you can figure out a way to make a fire."

"You can cook?"

"Yes." She raised her head to look at him. "Why do you sound so surprised?"

"I don't know. Maybe Naessa is different than Silvershire. I would have thought you had your own army of chefs, ready to make whatever exotic dish you fancied."

"Not in my household. I live alone, and like it that way."

"Hmmm." The sound he made told her he didn't believe her. "I watch the news, read the papers. You grew up with every luxury money can buy. Your run with the elite upper crust."

"That was college." She smiled, trying to pretend she cherished the memory. "We've lost touch since then." The truth of the matter was, none of the wealthy friends who'd permitted her to hang with them could relate to her life now. Playing cello for the symphony was, as one jet-setting type had put it, boring. Endless practices and performances left no time for partying.

"Still," he persisted. "Your mother is in the news quite

often. You grew up with chefs, maids and butlers. I find it surprising you know how to cook."

"Even cooks get a day or two off. My mother liked to keep me busy. Until she packed me off to boarding school, I was my mother's personal chef." The instant she'd finished speaking, she realized what she'd said. More than she'd revealed to anyone about her childhood, ever. Including Reginald. Especially Reginald.

So why now? Why Chase, who was still a virtual stranger?

He cocked his head, regarding her with a speculative look. "Still, you're quite wealthy. You mentioned a trust fund earlier. Did your father set you up with that?"

Common knowledge, especially for someone in public relations. "Yes."

"But according to the press, you and your father aren't close."

"True." She dipped her chin. "The trust fund is the only thing my sire ever did for me. He has other children, by his wife. I don't know them."

"You never refer to him as father, always sire. Why?"

"He never was a father to me."

"Yet you're still his child, still the daughter of a prince. You must have something in common."

"Illegitimate daughter." She tried to keep the bitterness from her voice. "There's a big difference. Actually, I've never even met the man."

Then, because talking about it still hurt, even after all these years, she took a hesitant step forward. When her legs held, she tried another. Gaining confidence, she moved out from under their shelter and crashed off through the underbrush into the shadowy forest.

"Where are you going?" he called after her.

"To gather more firewood." She tossed the lie over her shoulder.

After a moment, Chase followed. "Sydney, I—"

"Seriously, I'd rather be alone. Shouldn't you be fishing or hunting or something?"

He came up alongside her, moving so swiftly and quietly he startled her. He grabbed her arm. Annoyed, she stopped and glared up at him. He'd moved so fast she hadn't been able to avoid him. His face was in shadow, making it difficult to read his expression.

"You're right. I should be fishing or hunting." But he made no move to go.

Absurdly, she wanted to hurl herself into his arms and let him hold her while she cried. She looked at him, tried to speak, and found herself sobbing.

He made the move to gather her close. "Shh."

Stiffly, she let him hold her while she cried. Would being in a man's arms always be her salvation? She wasn't her mother.

At that thought, she pushed herself away from him. But he wouldn't let her go.

"It's all right. We've survived a plane crash. I know you're worried about your baby." His voice sounded calm, but she could hear his pounding heartbeat under her ear. His chest rose and fell with each breath, and she realized his arousal mirrored her own dawning awareness of him as a man.

"I…" Lifting her head, she saw desire blazing in his eyes, need harsh in his handsome face.

"Chase?" She froze.

"Adrenaline," he ground out the word. "Natural reaction. We're alive, after all, and we only feel the need to prove it."

Was he trying to convince her, or himself?

But he was right. Primitive, fierce desire shook her. Irrational, maybe, but she wanted him. Boldly, she skimmed her hands up his muscular chest. He responded with a sharp intake of breath. Moving closer, as though she'd climb inside him if she could, she felt his arousal against her belly and shuddered.

Standing on tiptoe, she pressed a whispery kiss against his throat, tasting the salt of his sweat on his skin.

"Sydney?" He sounded like a man in torment. "Be careful what you start."

But she couldn't think, couldn't rationalize. Urgency driving her, she tilted her head back and looked up at him, letting him read her own need in her face. "Kiss me, Chase. Now."

With a half groan, half oath, he complied. Demanding, he covered her mouth with his, using his tongue to force her lips apart so he could enter.

Her arousal grew as his pirate's kiss plundered her mouth.

Lost in a fog of desire, at first she didn't react when he pushed her away, holding her at arm's length.

"If we do this now, we'll be sorry for it later." His dark look told her he already regretted things had gone so far. But his body—his magnificent, fully aroused body—told her differently.

She swallowed hard, her chest rising and falling with each jagged breath. Part of her wanted to fling herself at him, knowing he wouldn't be able to resist a second time.

But luckily, rationality conquered desire, and she nodded. "You can let me go," she said, her voice tight and controlled, though her body still tingled. "I promise I won't touch you again."

His pulse beat in his throat. He held her gaze for a long moment, his hands still on her arms, so close she could feel the heat radiate from his body.

"Don't make promises you can't keep." With that, he released her, striding off toward the shoreline. For one absurd moment she thought of chasing after him. Instead, she stayed in the shadowy woods, watching him with her heart in her throat and wondered what had happened to her pride.

Chapter 4

Sydney gathered as many sticks as she could find, knowing they could always use more firewood, while keeping her eye out for berries or anything recognizably edible.

She wanted to go home, to her townhouse in Tice, on Naessa's western shore. She wanted her own doctor, a thorough examination, then a huge dinner of pasta and bread.

Since none of those things were immediately forthcoming, she concentrated on what she could have. A meal of freshly caught fish or wild game. A way to get through an uncomfortable evening with a man who both despised and desired her.

And she felt the same, God only knew why.

Shaking her head, she continued gathering wood and prayed rescue would come soon, before she disgraced herself even further.

Later, when he returned with two dead rabbits dangling

from his hands, she eyed the poor things and nearly gagged. It was one thing to think about eating wild game and another thing entirely to have to actually do it.

Something must have shown on her face.

"Remember, you have to eat. After all, you're eating for two," he said.

"I know." She pointed to her impressive pile of sticks. "How are you at starting fires?"

He frowned. "I don't think rubbing two sticks together will work without flint. Or," he reached in his pocket with his free hand, "I can use this." He held up a silver lighter, flashing a grin.

After a moment of stunned amazement—he was so damn beautiful when he smiled—Sydney shook her head and chuckled, too. "I didn't know you smoked."

"I don't. I found this near the wreckage. It must have belonged to Franco or Dell."

Soon he had a small fire going. Despite her initial misgivings, the wild hare tasted better than she'd expected, and she finished hers quickly, licking the remaining fat from her fingers.

They sat in companionable silence, watching the bright orange sun sink toward the horizon. Clouds were gathering to the west, dark ominous clouds, making her shiver.

"There's a storm brewing out over the ocean." Chase must have seen her looking. "We can only hope it will miss us."

A storm. Sydney shivered. Already she could smell the scent of rain in the air. The atmosphere fairly buzzed with electricity. *Great.* She'd promised not to touch him again, and all she could think was how much safer she'd feel in his arms.

Chase Savage. A man she barely knew.

A quick glance at him, relaxing on his elbows by their

small fire, told her he was completely unaware of her irrational fear. She studied his muscular arms and long legs, and pushed away a stab of desire.

In the distance, thunder rumbled.

Heart pounding, she jumped to her feet.

He looked up in surprise. "Where're you going?"

Carefully, she avoided looking at him. "For a walk, I think."

"Don't be gone too long." He went back to watching the fire. "That storm will be here in less than an hour."

Hesitating, she thought about telling him of her fear, the sharp terror that overtook her in the midst of a storm. But knowing he'd believe the worst of her no matter what she said, she held her tongue and moved off down the beach. Skimming rocks into the waves, she watched the storm march closer across the sky and trembled, trying to conquer her anxiety

Scooping up a flat stone, she aimed and flipped her wrist. Another rock hit the ocean with a plop. She hadn't ever gotten the hang of skimming them across the water either.

Dry-eyed, chest aching, she looked over her shoulder at the small fire. In the dim light of dusk, she could just barely make out his silhouette, now sitting upright, adding sticks to the flames.

Alone.

To paraphrase one of her mother's favorite country and western songs, she felt so lonesome she could cry.

She shouldn't feel like this—after all, she was used to being by herself. Solitary. When she'd been a child, her own mother had refused to hold her. Sydney had gotten what comfort she could from an endless parade of nannies. After losing one too many beloved nannies, she had retreated into her own newfound shell. Comfortable there, she'd believed she'd made a good life, a safe life, insulated from hurt. She'd believed she was happy.

Until Prince Reginald had come along. Then, with his honeyed words and silken touch, he'd made her realize there was more to life than simply existing. A few months of his false adoration, and the walls she'd so carefully constructed around herself had crumbled, allowing a surprisingly passionate woman to emerge from the ruins.

Now, in the process of learning to rebuild those damned walls, just for tonight she longed to rip them away and toss them into the ocean.

None of this made sense.

So she walked and tossed rocks and, as the sky darkened and the sound of thunder grew louder, trembled and tried to figure out what she was going to do.

Chase waited until it was nearly dark to go look for her. Then, irritation fueled by frustration, he went after her.

For a woman who'd been Prince Reginald's plaything, passion certainly appeared to surprise Sydney Conner. Of course, this could all be a game to her, a way to amuse herself until they were rescued and she could return to her manicures and designer clothing. Chase's experience had taught him beautiful women were like that.

But Sydney seemed…different. More innocent, somehow. Shaking his head, Chase snorted. Kayla had convinced him she was different, too, once upon another life. He'd even believed her when she'd told him the baby she'd carried was his. He'd vowed to be careful whom he trusted after he'd learned Kayla had lied.

Careful? Once again, he burned for a woman. He desired Sydney Conner. Plain and simple. Even knowing she'd been the prince's lover and carried Reginald's baby, he wanted her.

He kept to the shelter of the trees, and the first raindrops splattered the leaves as the outer edge of the storm reached the island. Lightning flashed and thunder rumbled across the dark sky, briefly reminding him of the horrific moments before the royal jet had crashed.

Where was Sydney?

The next flash of lightning illuminated her, running toward the forest over the rocky beach. The rain began to pelt him in earnest as he took off for her. They met halfway, which told him she'd seen him at the same time he'd seen her.

Some old television commercial with two people leaping into each other's arms flashed into his mind. Damn, he had it bad. He forced himself to slow his pace.

Drenched, they skidded to a stop in front of each other. Eyes wide and haunted, she pushed her soaked hair away from her face and wrapped her arms around her thin waist.

Chase cleared his throat. "Are you all right?"

She nodded. "Yes, I think so. I have this thing about storms."

"Follow me." He had to shout to be heard over the roar of the downpour.

They ran through the deluge, lightning flashing all around them. The wind drove the rain in sheets, making it difficult to see. When they reached the shelter, he was relieved to see it still stood, despite the storm's fury.

At the entrance, she hesitated, glancing back at him while water ran down her face in rivulets. "I—"

"Come on." Hand in the small of her back, he helped her inside. Out of the rain, the small space felt warmer.

"How long do you think this storm will last?" The tremor in her voice could have been because she was cold.

"It's huge. This is just the leading edge. I think the waves will surge, so it's a good thing we're sheltered up here, away from the beach."

Still as a statue, she stood motionless in the dark, dripping and shivering. Only a few feet separated them. He wanted to wrap her in his arms and let their combined body heat warm them, but hesitated. "Are you all right?"

"We're surrounded by metal," she said, teeth chattering. "Is it safe to be here while there's lightning?"

The rain beat steadily on the metal roof, but the rough structure held. "Safer than outside in that storm."

He could have sworn he heard her whimper low in her throat. "Sydney?"

Pulling his lighter from his pocket, he clicked it on. In the second of light the flame provided, he saw her pale, pinched face, the terror in her dilated eyes. "You're really frightened."

She made a strangled sound of assent.

He fought the urge to take her in his arms. "Don't be afraid."

"I have a thing about storms," she told him, her voice shaking. "Once, when I was a child, I was in a sailboat during a storm. The boat capsized. I almost drowned. Since then, I've always been terrified of them."

Ah, damn. One step closed the distance between them. Telling himself he would offer only comfort, he gathered her close. Violent tremors shook her and, soaked and bedraggled, her sleek skin felt like ice.

"It's all right," he murmured, sinking to the ground, his arms full of drenched woman, trying to warm her the only way he could.

Her shivers had become great shudders. She clung to him with a desperation that touched him, despite all he knew about her.

"I'm sorry." Her apology was low, her voice full of shame. "I'm so damn cold…"

He began to try and warm her in earnest, though he imagined the touch of his callused fingers felt downright sacrilegious as he rubbed them over her soft skin. The silky softness of her wet body, the curve and perfection of her form, told how far out of his league he was with a woman like her.

But she needed him now and, no matter what else he might have become, he would always have some bodyguard in him.

He prayed she wasn't aware of how much she turned him on.

Apparently not. Oblivious, head against his chest, she continued to tremble and clutch at him, gasping out loud when another crack of thunder and flash of lightning shook the earth.

"Shh." Attempting to soothe her, he continued to try and thaw her, to rub warmth back into her frozen limbs, while ignoring the heat that rose in him at the feel of her wrapped around him.

Disgusted with himself, he grabbed the lap blanket he'd salvaged from the wreckage and handed it to her.

"Get out of your wet clothes." His voice sounded like rusty nails. He prayed she wouldn't notice.

"Now? Here?" Her shocked tone made him smile, glad she couldn't see him in the darkness.

Gently, he eased her from his lap, and shifted to lessen the pressure brought on by his growing arousal. "Yes, here. Use the blanket to dry off. Then wrap up in it."

"Good idea." A moment later, the sound of her unzipping her ragged slacks had him gritting his teeth. Images of Sydney, sleek and naked in his arms, tormented him, adding to his physical discomfort.

Feeling like a voyeur, he listened as she peeled off her wet blouse, and held his breath as he imagined her unhooking her bra and freeing her lush breasts. He ached to reach out and cup them, so he clenched his hands into fists to keep from doing exactly that.

"There," she said, and sighed. "You're right. This blanket feels good. Much warmer."

He couldn't find his voice to answer, so he said nothing, listening to the storm, his heartbeat drumming in his ears, and the harsh sound of his uneven breathing.

Another crack of thunder, and the rain began to batter them. The accompanying flash of lightning showed Sydney, wrapped in the blanket and standing, body rigid, her eyes wide with silent terror.

Chase clenched his jaw. If he made it through this night without touching her, he should be awarded a medal.

"Come here," he told her, shifting to shield her from his raging erection. "Lie down and let me hold you."

"Thank you." She settled on the ground next to him.

Then, touching her with only his upper body, he wrapped his arm around her slender, blanket-wrapped shoulders, and wondered how the hell he was going to get any sleep.

Sydney opened her eyes, drowsy and comfortably warm. Outside, the storm still raged, but wrapped in Chase's muscular arms, her fear had vanished. The dim light told her morning had arrived.

And she was naked, curled up against his equally bare body. Instantly, she came awake, her heartbeat tripling.

Chase still slept, his chest rising with his deep and even breathing. With one arm, he kept her close to him, tucked spoonlike against him. Twisting slowly in his arms, she lay on her back and studied him. Even asleep, he was beautiful. The stubble on his chin made him look even more masculine, even more sexy.

She had no urge to move, nowhere to go. Content to watch him, she tried to figure out her own admittedly skewed logic. She and Chase. A man she barely knew, who'd made it quite plain what he thought of her.

If it weren't so damn pitiful, she'd laugh. Chalk one up to feeling extremely vulnerable. Not only did she consider her and her unborn baby's survival a miracle, but her companion on this deserted island was a drop-dead-gorgeous and sexy-as-hell man.

Another woman might have found this heaven. Sydney tried to decide if she was in hell. The last thing she—or her child—needed was another disastrous relationship.

It might have been better if she'd demanded he make her another shelter, but the truth of the matter was that she didn't want to be alone.

No, if she was being totally honest, the simple reality was she craved his kiss, his touch, his smile.

Chase.

When he touched her she felt like the most desirable woman on earth.

She was an idiot: lying here naked while her clothes, surely dry by now, lay within arm's reach of their makeshift bed.

But berating herself did little good. She was only human after all. Every time he shifted his body, she felt the movement vibrate along her nerve endings, straight to the inner core of her. The storm-moist air caressed her bare skin, and she felt hypersensitive. Everything—the rustle of the leaves underneath them, the rise and fall of his chest, his masculine scent, the way his tousled blond hair fell across his forehead—aroused her as she'd never been before.

He turned, still sleeping, and muttered something, too low for her to understand at first. A name? While she tried to puzzle that, he snuggled against her, his perfectly formed body pressed against the full length of hers. For an instant, she forgot to breathe.

Good Lord, how she wanted this man!

Tentatively, she stretched, rubbing herself against him like a starving cat. Her entire body tingled. Her breasts were tender and aching, and her pulse beat hot and heavy in places she'd never known it could.

Ah, temptation. One heartbeat away from continuing to move her body against him while he slept, she tried desperately to remember the reasons she shouldn't. But all she could think about was how badly she wanted to stroke him, caress him, and take him beyond the bounds of his control before he woke and rationality set in. A veritable feast of man sprawled out before her, Chase unknowingly lured her to do things she'd never before done, even with Reginald. She'd placed her hand against his chest and begun to trace it lower before she realized she'd moved.

Horrified, she froze. What was wrong with her? Yes, she was attracted to him. He was the most beautiful man she'd ever seen. What red-blooded woman wouldn't be?

But she wasn't like this. Sydney had always been different. Once, only once, had she given in to impulse and let Reginald's lies persuade her to his bed. And now she carried his child, the baby of another beautiful man who'd broken her heart.

Had she learned nothing from her mistake? Having been a fool once, was she doomed to act foolishly forever?

"Sydney?"

Her breath caught. With a gasp, she removed her hand from him. "Yes?"

"You're awake," he said, his voice husky with sleep or, she shivered, desire. His hazel eyes roamed over her, reminding her she was still naked, stretched out seductively, as if she'd been waiting for him to wake and make love to her.

In a way, she had.

Feeling her face heat, she rolled away and grabbed for her clothes. The tattered shorts, once her favorite pair of slacks, were still damp. She pulled them on anyway.

"Yes. The storm woke me," she said, struggling to yank her mostly dry blouse over her head.

Never taking his eyes from her, he sat up, dragging his hand through his hair. One corner of his mouth quirked in a smile. "Some storm. I'm glad this shelter held."

Even fully clothed, her heart still raced like a runaway rabbit. She cleared her throat. "So far, so good. Not even a single leak."

His gaze dropped lower, to her breasts, where her nipples pushed rebelliously against her ragged shirt. He gave a harsh intake of breath, his eyes darkening.

She couldn't help but wonder if he was as turned on as she.

No way was she finding out. Knowing how volatile the situation could become, she climbed to her feet and crossed her arms.

He tilted his head, squinting up at her. "Are you all right?"

"I'm fine." Her need still pulsed within her, making her ache. She tucked a wayward strand of hair behind her ear, wishing she could think of something to say, something to diffuse the fierce sexual tension making the air feel so heavy.

Chase sat up, drawing the blanket close and carefully wrapping it around him.

"Sydney, don't." Though husky, his voice sounded tight, controlled, much like the man himself most of the time. If not for the hunger in his eyes, she'd think him unaffected. "Don't try to seduce me."

Seduce him? If he only knew how badly she wanted to and how hard she'd tried to resist him. She swallowed. "I'm not."

Narrowing his gaze, he raked his hand through his hair. He looked away and cursed. "I don't know what it is about you. I even see the promise of sex in your smile."

"Sex in my smile?" Though she tossed his words back at him, a thrill ran through her at his words. "That sounds lovely, but it's ridiculous. I've done nothing to entice you. I wouldn't know how! I've never tried to seduce anyone in my life."

He clenched his jaw and got to his feet, keeping the damn blanket snug around his waist. "But you have. Maybe you don't realize it, but everything about you is a seduction. The way you move, the way you toss your head. Your smile, your voice…" Cursing under his breath, he took a step toward her and stopped, hands clenched at his sides. "You'd tempt a dead man straight into hell."

"I—"

"I'm not finished. When I first saw you, I wondered. You weren't Reginald's usual type. But now I can better understand what the prince saw in you."

Reginald. Hearing that name was like a dash of cold

water. If Chase had wanted to hurt her, he'd succeeded admirably. Together, she and Reginald had created another life, and he'd spurned her. Not just her, but all of it. The man hadn't wanted his own child. Exactly as her sire hadn't wanted her.

She should be used to rejection, honestly. But that didn't stop it from hurting. Hot tears stung the back of her throat. Damn hormones. She turned away, fist to her mouth.

Behind her, Chase snarled. "One mention of Reginald and that's enough to bring you to tears? Did you truly care for him that much?"

He sounded furious. And hurt. Which was impossible. Either way, Sydney knew she shouldn't care. Didn't care. Hell, she *wouldn't* care.

The rain had picked up again, mirroring her mood. On the edge of losing her fragile grip on self-control, she didn't answer. Couldn't answer, when it came right down to it.

"Who are you, Sydney Conner?" His hoarse voice told her he'd moved up behind her. He touched her shoulder, his hand impossibly gentle, and turned her to face him, pulling her close to his chest. Though she didn't resist, she let him hold her, keeping herself rigid. Silently, he stroked her hair, while she fought back tears that came for no good reason.

"Go ahead and cry."

Those four words, muttered against her hair by a man she suspected would rather miss every target on the firing range than soothe a weeping woman, pushed her over the edge.

She cried while he held her, this stranger who wasn't a stranger, not any longer. Nearly dying in a plane crash and being stuck together on a deserted island had made him feel familiar. Intimately.

Her tears soaked his bare chest. Bare, muscular, hard

chest. Dimly, this registered and, as her weeping subsided, she found herself longing to move the hand pressed against him. To splay her fingers, to stroke him slowly, to allow herself to indulge in all that masculinity right there under her fingertips.

His comment about seduction hadn't been that far off the mark.

Good Lord! Had she truly become her mother? Gone totally over the edge? Though she'd already made one mistake her mother had made, she vowed she wouldn't make another. If her affair with Reginald had made her this way, she needed to get back to the woman she'd been before.

This didn't make her desire for him disappear, or even lessen. She still craved his touch, somehow addicted to something she'd never even had.

Hah! If he'd thought she'd been trying to seduce him before, what would he think if she gave in to her irrational need to caress him?

She wouldn't. She'd made enough mistakes to last her entire twenty-four years, Reginald chief among them. She didn't need to make one more.

Hiccuping, she sniffed and pushed herself away. "Sorry about that." She wouldn't look at him, her feminine vanity not wanting him to see her no doubt bright-red nose and swollen eyes.

He muttered something that sounded like "That's okay."

Though she waited, he made no move to leave, even though the drumming of the rain had all but stopped.

Wiping at her eyes, she managed a watery smile and gave the doorway a pointed look. "I don't know about you, but I'm starving. The rain's letting up. How about we go outside and forage for some breakfast?"

"What?" he stared at her as if he thought she'd lost her mind. "It's barely dawn."

"I'm pregnant," she said crossly, then smiled to soften the sting of her tone. "Not only am I changing the subject, but I really am hungry."

Crossing his arms, he swallowed. "You know, I keep forgetting you're pregnant."

One deep breath, then another. Soon, maybe her erratic heartbeat would slow down to normal. "It's too soon for me to show." Patting her still-flat abdomen, she grimaced. "Give it a few months. I've had so little time to actually enjoy my pregnancy. Every little girl dreams of the day when she'll be pregnant and become a mommy."

"Even a princess?"

She could see him relaxing in stages. "Yes, even a princess. I wanted to be able to luxuriate in it, wallow in it, you know? Instead, I'm trapped on an island with little food and no—"

"Luxuries." He sounded so hard and so certain, she blinked.

"That's not what I was going to say. I was thinking more of people. Friends that care."

The look he gave her was skeptical. "Don't tell me you don't miss the life you had in Naessa. You made the papers often, you know. Your lifestyle was no secret. I saw your townhouse on the coast on that TV show. You lived like royalty."

If only he knew. She'd filled her home with beautiful things, trying to fill the emptiness inside her. She'd been lonely more often than not, especially when she wasn't traveling with the symphony.

But he didn't know that. No one did. "I confess to missing some of it, yes."

"What?" His voice was fierce, and his hazel eyes darkened. "Which do you miss most? The Egyptian cotton sheets? The fine restaurants? Or the chance to have Frost and French design your maternity clothes?"

"You know about them?"

"I'm in public relations. I have to keep up with the trends. Answer my question. Which do you miss the most?" He took a step closer, his face intent.

Heart caught in her throat, she stared at him.

He leaned close, and for one heart-stopping moment she thought he was going to kiss her. Worse, she knew if he did, this time she wouldn't pull away.

Chapter 5

Luckily for both of them, he caught himself in time.

Clearing her throat, she searched desperately for something to say to pretend she hadn't noticed. Outside, the rain had slowed to a light patter on their metal roof.

"I really do miss my friends," she said, inanely. "What about you?"

He shrugged.

"Since your business takes you out and about, I imagine you must have a large circle of friends."

"Not really." He rolled his shoulders before snagging his own shirt and slipping it on. Apparently he was as eager as she to act as if nothing had happened. "My job consumes most of my day. I have little time to maintain friendships outside of my work. However, my coworkers and I get along well, and of course, there's always my family. Your turn."

For a second she didn't understand, eyeing him blankly.

"Are you close to your family?" He stepped into his shorts.

Her mouth went dry. Averting her eyes, she attempted to swallow while listening to the rasp of the denim. "My family?"

"Yes."

"No." She shook her head, trying to focus on the question. The only family she had was her mother, which equaled no family at all. "I'm not. I assume you are?"

"Oh, yeah. My parents live near the west coast of Silvershire, in their dream retirement home. My brothers and sisters are all married and have children. We all get together several times a year."

Finally, she regained her senses, though the entire conversation still seemed surreal. "I always wished for a big family."

"I read you're an only child."

"Yes." Since her mother had felt having Sydney had ruined her life, the woman had taken steps to ensure she didn't have any more children. "But I made a lot of friends in the symphony."

At her mention of her job, Chase grimaced. "I bet you're glad now that you left your cello in the hotel. That thing wouldn't have survived the crash. At least this way, you have a chance of getting it back."

"True. If it's still there."

"That was a five-star hotel. I'm sure they have your instrument in their lost and found department."

"As long as no one realizes it's a Strad, it's probably okay. Otherwise, they'd sell it on the black market." She gave him a tentative smile, finally feeling normal. "Right about now I should be back in Naessa, getting ready for Silvershire's Founder's Day celebration. We rehearse every night for a month. This will be my third performance for your king."

At the mention of the celebration, Chase frowned. "Given the bad blood between your father and King Weston, I'm surprised Naessa's symphony was invited this year."

Lifting her chin, she forced her mouth to curve in what she hoped resembled a smile. "I've always heard the fish bite better at dawn. Is there any truth to that?"

"Changing the subject?"

"Yes," she said, her voice mild. "I'm still hungry."

He gave a half bow. "Which would you prefer? Fish or rabbit?"

"*Do* the fish bite better at dawn?"

"Maybe. I guess I'll go out there and find out. I take it you'd like fish for breakfast?"

Her lower back ached. Absently, she rubbed it while she pondered his question. "We had rabbit last night." She had to smile at her words.

"What?" Chase caught the smile.

"Listen to us, talking about eating wild game as though discussing the menu at Chez Niablo." She sighed. "I need protein, lots of it, for the baby. I feel the need for fish."

"Then fish it is. Catch." He tossed her the lighter. "Why don't you see about making a fire while I get our breakfast?" Then, without a backward glance, he left.

Surprised she'd caught the lighter since she'd lifted her hand in reflex, Sydney closed her fist over it. The silver metal felt both foreign and reassuringly normal. She turned to the small pile of wood he'd brought inside the shelter and gathered an armful before stepping cautiously outside.

Though still overcast, the sky looked considerably brighter. With the light mist and soft breeze, the still-dripping forest smelled earthy and fresh. The storm had gone. Shrouded in clouds, the small hill they'd dubbed Haystack Mountain could be seen clearly.

Three tries and Sydney finally had a respectable fire going. She fed the flames dry wood, and glanced toward the beach, trying to catch a glimpse of Chase in the waves.

While she watched the fire and waited, she thought of how drastically her life had changed in a few days. Now, with her existence pared down to survival, simple pleasures like the warmth of a fire or the feel of a man's rough stubble against her cheek seemed more precious than diamonds.

Finally, Chase returned, carrying not only two large fish, but what looked like a battered backpack.

"I went poking through more of the wreckage." He placed the backpack on the ground. "I found this. It must have belonged to one of the pilots."

She noticed he avoided saying their names and realized that must be his way of dealing with his grief. So instead of commenting, she focused on the fish.

"How long will that take to cook?"

He smiled. "I thought you said you knew how."

Unembarrassed, she shrugged. "I learned how to cook gourmet meals using an oven. If cooking over an open fire is similar, then I'm good to go."

"Let me show you." Using the same rig he'd made to cook the rabbits, he spread the fish over the fire.

They watched in companionable silence while their breakfast cooked. Every so often, he turned the spit.

Finally, he gave her a satisfied look. "I think it's done."

Removing the fish from the fire, he split each in half, using a triangular rock as a cutting implement. Then he transferred her portion to a piece of bark and handed it to her.

"You're pretty handy with nature," she commented.

"I trained at a pretty elite bodyguard school in Carringtonshire." Taking a bite of his fish, he pointed to hers. "Now eat."

Aching again, Sydney complied. "It's good."

"You sound surprised." He'd wolfed down his portion before she'd even finished chewing.

"I guess I am." Chewing slowly, she savored the flavor. "Even without the benefit of seasonings or spices, this is wonderful. It's flaky and moist." Though she'd eaten at gourmet restaurants in both their countries, she thought she'd never tasted anything so delicious.

"It's fresh."

It took her a moment to realize he was teasing her. She eyed him, his rugged face relaxed, and replied in kind. "It'd be even better if I didn't have to pick out the bones."

Chase grinned. "Tough," he told her. "There are some things you have to do on your own."

Finishing her portion, she licked her fingers to get every bit of meat. When she looked up again, Chase's lighthearted expression had vanished. His look burned her all the way to her core.

"Chase—"

"No." He jumped to his feet and took her bark from her, dumping the fish bones in the fire. Then, without a backward look, he strode off into the forest.

After a moment of hesitation, she ran after him. "Where are you going?"

He cast a dark look over his shoulder. "In lieu of a cold shower, I'm going to take a bath in the pond."

She practically had to jog to keep up with him. "I'd kill for some soap."

Hefting the backpack, he kept going. "I found some."

"Soap?" She felt like Eve, being lured with a different kind of apple. "Is there enough for both of us?"

"I'd prefer to bathe alone, thank you." He gave her another hard look. "I'll bring back the soap so you can have a turn."

She stopped, letting him continue on alone. He was right. Thoughts of him emerging naked from the pond with rivulets of water caressing his muscular body was way more temptation than she was up to resisting.

And resist she must. Because, unless their rescuers made an appearance, they'd spend another night sleeping side by side in the small shelter. She had to stop thinking of him that way before they both did something they'd later regret.

On the way back to the camp, she took a detour and found a patch of early strawberries. Going back for the tin cups Chase had found earlier, she returned to fill them with strawberries.

Bare-chested, hair damp from his swim, Chase returned and handed her the soap. "I'll see you later."

Resolutely, she kept her gaze on his face. "Where are you going?"

He seemed just as determined to avoid looking below her chin. "I thought I'd climb Haystack Mountain and see if I could get a better visual on this island."

Though it was on the tip of her tongue to ask to go, she didn't. Instead, she nodded and took off for the pond and her own bath. She didn't turn around to see if he watched her leave.

That night, he brought them a small wild pig. She'd gathered more wood, spreading it in the sun to dry before hauling a short stack inside the shelter in case of more rain. While he dressed the meat, she built up the fire. Though she hadn't seen him all day, she kept her distance while he cooked their dinner on another stick-made spit.

The scent of roasting pork made her mouth water and finally, she went closer. "That smells wonderful."

He nodded. "I re-explored the wreckage hoping to find a working cell phone or radio or something. Instead, I found the remains of the galley." He held up two forks. "I brought back these and those plastic food trays to use as plates."

Feeling absurdly tongue-tied, she looked away.

"I also found an underground route to some caves." He brushed back his hair from his face.

"Caves?"

"This is an interesting island. Below the pond is a lot of volcanic rock. There were a couple of large caves, accessible only by water. When I get more time, I'll explore them." He fed another stick to the fire. "What'd you do while I was gone?"

"I picked a bunch of berries and gathered firewood." She sighed. "I also took a nap. I've been really tired today."

"Isn't that normal?" Turning the spit while he watched her, his expression was unreadable.

"For pregnant women, yes."

"I climbed Haystack and got a better view of this place." He gestured toward the beach. "It's not a huge island, and I didn't see any signs of habitation. I did find a sandy beach on the other side, rather than this rocky one we're near. The wildlife is abundant—even with me crashing around in broad daylight I saw a lot." His teeth flashed white. "Not a bad place to build a vacation home. I haven't figured out why the owner hasn't yet."

Sydney nodded. Just looking at him made her ache. His blond hair was sun-streaked, though she wondered how much time he spent in the sun, back in Silvershire. With his darkened tan and his stubble, he looked even more dangerous than he had before.

And more sexy.

Her stomach growled, bringing her thoughts back to food. "How much longer?"

"I think it's about done." Moving the cooked pig to a rock, he made good use of a steak knife to cut up their meat. Handing her a plate, he filled his and retreated to the other side of the fire to eat.

Sydney felt as though he was drawing a battle line.

Instead of worrying about that, she concentrated on her food. They ate in silence.

When they'd finished, eating almost all of the small pig, Chase dug a hole and buried the remains.

Once he'd finished, he returned to his side of the fire.

Night fell suddenly. Stars flickered above in the velvet-black sky. Across from her, separated by the dancing flames, Chase used the steak knife to carve another stick to use as a spit.

Sydney tried to enjoy the quiet, listening to the night sounds of the forest as the myriad creatures emerged to hunt and play. All her life, she'd been so excruciatingly lonely that silence had been intolerable to her. Until she'd learned to play the cello. After that, she'd always managed to fill the quiet with her music.

Now, without her cello, once again she sat alone. On the outside looking in. Only when she played with the symphony did she feel part of something larger, no longer solitary in her insulated little world.

Sitting across the fire from this hard man, she felt even more alone than when Reginald's gaze had slid dismissively over her in a crowded restaurant. Reginald, once so blatant in his adoration, had pretended not to know her.

Chase made no such pretense. He simply preferred not to talk.

She recognized this. Years and years of living on the outside of the "inside" people, had trained her for it. How not to interfere or intrude. How to make certain her existence didn't impede or alter their lives in any unpleasant way.

Her mother had taught her well.

But this wasn't Naessa and she wasn't a child. So—she took a deep breath—she wouldn't put up with it again. Not here. Not now. Not ever again. She spoke.

"Do you think someone will find us?"

Barely pausing in his carving, he turned those amazing hazel eyes of his to hers. "Yes."

"Why do you sound unhappy about that?"

He stabbed the knife into the ground. "Do I? I'm not, not at all. I'm hoping the right people find us first."

"The right people?"

"The ones who are on our side."

She hadn't thought of that until now. Cradling her stomach and the growing life within, she tried to picture these people and shook her head. She still wasn't sure if they were a figment of Chase's imagination, or real, nameless, faceless enemies. There had been the shooting, certainly, but nothing had ever happened to her until Chase had shown up. They could be his enemies more than hers.

Except *her* car had been blown up. Hers, not his.

If there was someone out there gunning for them, it would seem it was really her they were after.

But why? Did they hate her merely because she carried Reginald's child? Or was it because of her ties to

Prince Kerwin of Naessa? Perhaps they were unaware her sire had never acknowledged her, though how they could be when it'd been trumpeted from every tabloid, she had no idea.

Even a few months ago, when the largest one had done a feature on her and Reginald, her bastard status had been mentioned, along with the speculation about whether, if she and Reginald were to wed, her father might consent to legitimize her.

The same paper had been the first to report on Reginald's intentions to honor his long-term betrothal to Princess Amelia Victoria DuPont of Gastonia. It seemed they'd been betrothed as toddlers in a secret agreement between King Weston of Silvershire and King Roman of Gastonia, a betrothal Reginald had conveniently forgotten to mention to Sydney. He planned to marry the princess during his coronation ceremony, which he'd ordered to be the most lavish the people of Silvershire had ever seen.

The same morning the story broke, Sydney had learned she was pregnant with Reginald's child.

"Surely it won't come to that. We've been missing, what, three days? Your duke must be looking for us."

"I'm sure he is. But then, so are they."

She glanced back at their small shelter. "We don't have any weapons."

"Not a one."

"Maybe we'd better find another place to hide."

"That's why I went up the mountain. If the wrong people show up, we'll need somewhere to ambush them."

His words only served to remind her how precious life could be and how abruptly it could be cut short.

Unable to bear the isolation any longer, Sydney rose.

Hugging herself, she moved around the fire and dropped to the ground next to Chase.

His mouth tightened, but he made no comment. The look he gave her was sharp and, for nameless reasons, touched a place deep inside her. But then, the way he affected her had nothing to do with reason.

Averting his face, he continued to work at whittling the stick. She studied him, memorizing his features, knowing that even once she returned to her normal life, she'd never forget a single detail of his face.

Reginald's good looks had been more patrician, elegant. More remote. She'd thought she'd loved him, but she realized now what she'd mistaken for love had been gratitude for attention. She'd been so hungry for affection that she'd turned a blind eye to all Reginald's failings. Knowing his reputation, she'd believed her love had changed him.

Loving Reginald had been her biggest mistake. Until now. Looking at Chase, at the stubborn set of his chin and his deliberate unawareness of her, she knew she was about to make another.

The fire crackled and popped. Around them, she could hear the night sounds of the forest, and the soft scratch Chase's knife made on the wood.

Soon, they'd let the fire burn down and retire for the evening. Soon, they'd lie side by side in their small shelter and try to pretend to be unaware of each other.

She was tired of resisting, tired of existing half-alive and so achingly alone. She wanted him. And he wanted her. After they were rescued, she'd go home to Naessa and never see him again. Until then, for however long they were stranded here, they only had each other.

Heart hammering in her chest, she took a deep breath

for courage. She touched his arm, bringing the heat of his shadowed gaze to her face. "Chase, I need to ask you something." Swallowing, she wished her voice wouldn't tremble so, or sound quite as breathy.

The knife stilled. Waiting for her to continue, he raised one golden brow.

Now or never. She felt as though she was diving, head-first, into a bottomless pool.

"Last night, when you held me, I felt better than I have in months. Less afraid, more secure. I liked feeling that way. A lot."

Ignoring his harsh intake of breath, she continued. "I want to sleep in your arms again tonight. Will you hold me through the night?"

Chapter 6

Did she know what she was asking of him? Chase couldn't believe what he was hearing. As Sydney stared at him, her slender fingers pale on his tanned arm, desire slammed into him like a punch to the gut. Gritting his teeth, he used every ounce of willpower to keep from yanking her hard against him, and covering her mouth with his.

Sydney had become an obsession.

Earlier, the way she'd watched him had been bad enough. He'd felt the touch of her luminous gaze like a silky caress, teasing his nerves to an aching awareness.

"Chase?" She scooted closer, filling his nostrils with the scent of warm, fragrant woman. He clenched his jaw. God help him if she were to move her hand from his arm and splay her fingers across his chest. She'd feel his heart thudding like a wild thing as he fought to keep himself under control.

She had no idea how much he wanted her. Wanted to

tangle his fingers in her hair and tilt her face to him. Wanted to feel her lush curves, full against him, without even small scraps of clothing acting as a barrier between them. Wanted to bury himself deep inside her and bring her to a ragged, shuddering completion as they moved together in a rhythm as old as time.

Ever since she'd turned that midnight-blue stare of hers on him, Chase had been battling himself. Now, with her so close, her lush mouth slightly parted, her long-lashed blue eyes dark with a desire that matched his own, he found her all but impossible to resist. His body quickened and he fought to keep from losing control.

Then her words penetrated his fogged brain.

She wanted to be held.

She'd asked in the way of one human asking another for comfort, not someone craving hot, wild sex.

Chase knew if he touched her, he'd do a lot more than hold her. He suspected Sydney realized this, as well.

Think of Kayla, he told himself savagely. Kayla had used his lust to blind him to her lies. And she hadn't had one-tenth the effect on him as Sydney.

Sydney. How he wanted her. Being around her made him feel as if a potent aphrodisiac had spread with lightning speed through his blood.

His control slipping, Chase tried to remember how Sydney had planned to use Reginald. Though Chase hadn't liked the man and even thought he'd deserved to pay the consequences for his actions, Sydney had to have known what she was getting into. No one was that naive. Or that successful.

Chase, like Reginald, knew a lion's share of gorgeous, sexy women. None could hold a candle to her.

Sydney Conner was sex on wheels.

But the question remained, what did she want from him?

Though she acted as though it was simple, human comfort, he knew better. She was beautiful, like Kayla. He had to believe beautiful women always had an agenda.

"Chase?" Even her voice, husky and sensual, seduced him. The mere act of hearing her say his name made him take an unthinking step toward her. "What is it? What's wrong?"

He had to stop this. Get a grip on his famous iron control. He could do this. He was a pro at handling sexy, beautiful women. With all his experiences, he hadn't lived the life of a monk after all. Resisting even the most sensual woman, while difficult, was doable.

Then he made the mistake of looking at her.

Sydney continued to stare up at him, her heart-shaped face breathtakingly vulnerable, her eyes so dark, pupil and iris appeared to have blended. He searched her expression for the particular confidence sexy women had, that innate knowledge that they could wrap a man, any man, around their little fingers. But either Sydney was different, or she was a damn fine actress. He saw nothing in her delicate features but a hint of sorrow, of pain, and a stark, lonely hunger that matched his own urgent need.

She wanted, he reminded himself savagely, to be held. So damn it, he'd hold her.

Somehow, without being conscious of moving, he found his hands on her, sliding across her soft skin, slipping up her arms. She made a sound, not of protest, not exactly, more of welcome, and he answered low in his throat.

Need, raw and sharp, clawed at him. Still, he made a heroic effort to keep himself from taking her, though she felt warm and supple and willing in his arms.

Willing. With a hoarse cry, he covered her mouth with

his. She met him halfway, lips parted, tongue mating. As before, the taste of her was sweet, like a nearly ripe peach.

When he pulled back, she made a soft mew of protest, pressing her body against him in a wordless plea. She touched her lips to his throat and he burned.

He heard another sound, realizing with a curious detachment it was the harsh, uneven rhythm of his own breathing. Or was it hers?

Was he crazy? Had he lost his mind? She was everything he ran from, everything Kayla had been and more.

And, as Kayla had been, she was pregnant with another man's child.

He gave himself a mental shake, which did nothing to lessen the heat in his blood. She reared back as his body stirred against her, her eyes wide and dark and her face clear, no artifice in her expression, just a sensual, womanly awareness. Awareness of the way her simple, quiet femininity called to him? Awareness of his body's raging hunger for her, only her?

Was she like Kayla had been, well aware that the lure she'd cast had reeled in yet another masculine conquest?

A second later he chastised himself for reading too much into her response. Sydney wasn't Kayla. She had her own motivations, her own needs. Perhaps she was only tired of being alone, apart, separate. Maybe, like him, she longed to touch, to make contact, to feel.

Maybe, she really needed him.

Him.

He knew a moment of wonder, then his innate cynicism set in. He was reacting to her like a sex-starved soldier, newly returned from the battlefield. Perhaps the sunlight had scrambled his brains. Or more likely it was the feel of her, all soft skin and womanly curves, but he tugged her closer, trying to be gentle when he wanted to be rough, comforting when he wanted the raw rhythm of hot, mindless sex.

She'd asked him merely to hold her, not make love to her. Was he reading too much into her words?

Yet she came to him, pressing herself against him for a moment, and as her curves molded to his body he knew he could take her there, on the ground near their fire, and slake his thirst deep inside her.

Hard, aching, he couldn't think, could barely stop himself from pushing against her, from laying her down and peeling off her clothes. He wanted to nuzzle her breasts, take her nipples into his mouth and taste her.

She made a soft sound and he found himself looking down at her. Her beautiful eyes were full of passion.

"Sydney?" Their gazes locked for the space of a heartbeat, and another. Without consciously willing it, Chase found himself claiming her mouth again.

The instant their lips touched, fire flared between them once more. He broke away, breathing hard, cursing his lack of willpower. She whimpered, and his body surged against her. She felt it, too, the infinitesimal change in his body as he fought to keep his raging arousal under control.

"What is it about you?" he growled, unable to make himself push her away. "Why are you doing this?"

With heavy-lidded eyes she looked up at him, her expression serious. He saw no hint of a tease or the simpering coquettishness he'd come to associate with the women who followed the royals, wanting sex. Rather, as she worried her bottom lip between her teeth, she looked as troubled as he felt.

Around them, the sound of surf pounding the rocks blended with his heartbeat.

Finally, she spoke. "I want you," she said. "But before I do, there's something you need to understand."

When he would have moved toward her, she held up her hand. "Reginald was my first."

Uncomprehending, he stared. "What?"

"I was a virgin before him. I've never been with anyone else. I thought he loved me, but he didn't. Now I'm pregnant."

Something inside him splintered. At her words he felt the rage leave him, an icy chill spreading through him instead. What he knew of Reginald's depravations could fill a book. For her first experience at lovemaking to have been at the hands of that...

Even for Reginald, this was a new low. Seduce a virgin, an illegitimate princess, impregnate her, then dump her to go off and marry a legitimate one. Though she gave no signs of knowing it, Sydney Conner was the most sexy, desirable woman Chase had ever met.

The possibility that she might be lying didn't make him feel any better.

"Sydney, I—" Oddly enough, her innocence only made him want her more.

He started toward her.

"Wait." She held up a hand, her delicate features remote. "I didn't tell you that to make you feel sorry for me. Actually, I'm not sure why I told you at all."

"I'm glad you did." He touched her shoulder and she looked up at him, her eyes full of unshed tears. All his resolve flew out the window. "I want you, Sydney. How I want you."

Her expression softened and she held out her arms.

"Then make love to me, Chase. Erase what he did to me from my memory. Make love to me."

Make love to me. He groaned. Despite his longing and the red-hot fantasies which haunted him, Chase knew he should back away.

Instead, he pulled her into his arms, slanting his mouth across hers. She met him halfway. He touched her, letting his hands roam over her curves freely, as he'd been aching to do. Her answering cry was a heady invitation.

Squirming against him, each movement acerbated the fierceness of his arousal, pushing him closer and closer to the edge of his ragged control.

"Chase," she spoke his name in a broken murmur, her lips against his throat. She trailed kisses there, making him shudder.

She didn't protest when he pulled off her blouse, nor when his fingers fumbled with the clasp of her bra. Then, when her breasts were free, he cupped them in his hands and suckled her, rolling each rosy nipple between his lips.

Arching her back, she moaned. Together, they sank to the ground. She found the waistband of his shorts and pulled the snap apart, finding him hard and swollen and spilling from his undershorts.

When she wrapped her hand around him and stroked, the movement brought pleasure and agony.

"Stop," he ground out. "You'll have me losing control too soon, too fast."

He pushed her back onto the sand, throbbing, hard, ready. With his finger he entered her, finding her wet and tight. She groaned. He readied himself between her legs, about to push into her, when a roaring sound filled the air.

"Chase?" She raised her head, a look of horror filling her face as she came to the same realization as he did.

Listening, he lifted himself up and cursed. "That's a chopper, landing on the beach. We need to hide until we know who it is."

In one swift motion he rolled off her, yanking up his shorts and helping her up and into her bra and T-shirt. "We're either about to be rescued or attacked."

Chapter 7

Together, they watched the chopper land on the rocky beach near where they'd buried the pig carcass. Before the whirring blades had even slowed, a tall, dark-haired man climbed out, followed by two others. Not only did the chopper look military, but the men appeared dangerous. All wore sunglasses, and she could see they were all armed with pistols. All of them were large men with the build of bodyguards.

"They look like bad guys." Sydney turned to Chase, still trying to adjust her clothing.

"Nope, they're not. We're in luck," Chase said, relief lightening the harshness in his eyes. "Those are my men, they work for me."

"Hell of a PR department you've got going." She eyed the weapons glinting in the sunlight. "Do you guys double as covert ops or something?"

Immediately, his expression shut down. "What we do—or don't do—in Silvershire has nothing to do with Naessa."

Once again, he reminded her she was an outsider.

"I understand." She matched his cool tone.

His gaze locked with hers. Another time, she might have found it amusing that Chase looked away first. Now, she felt only an awful ache spreading inside her heart. Despite that, when he held out his hand, she took it.

Fingers laced together, they ran across the sand, Chase shouting out one of the other men's names as they ran.

Twenty minutes later, the pilot put the chopper down at a place she didn't recognize.

The airstrip appeared to be private, with the helicopter's landing pad clearly marked.

Chase stayed by Sydney's side, helping her climb out from the chopper. A white Hummer limousine waited. With the other men leading the way, they bypassed this, heading for a small, unimpressive brick building. Inside, they stepped into an empty room furnished only with a single desk and a folding metal chair. A door marked Women was at one end; Men was at the other.

"Here you'll find showers and all the necessities, as well as some new clothing." The husky man Chase had introduced as William pointed to two suitcases. One, a small Gucci looked familiar, her favorite traveling bag.

"That's mine," she said. "Where did you get that?"

"Before his death, Prince Reginald had given us all the things you'd left at his flat, asking that we return them to you."

"Us?"

William looked at Chase. Gaze locked on Sydney, Chase nodded slowly. "Go ahead."

William flashed her an impersonal smile. "The royal public relations department. Us. We took the liberty of bringing your clothing, as well as of purchasing a few new items for your stay."

Alarm bells went off. "Stay?"

This time they all looked at Chase. He murmured, "Why don't you get cleaned up, then we'll talk."

Talk? About what? "I need to see a doctor before I do anything," she insisted.

Expressionless, he surveyed her. "Clean up first. Then we'll take you to a specialist for a thorough examination."

"But—"

"There's no doctor here, Sydney." Chase touched her arm. "Get cleaned up, change your clothes and we'll go. You'll feel a lot better if you do."

"What about my cello?"

He held up a finger. "Later, okay?"

Slowly, she nodded.

"I'll be right there if you need anything." He pointed to the other door. "William, Carlos and Jim will stand guard outside."

Stand guard? Didn't anyone else find it odd that Silvershire had a PR department made up of bodyguards? Shaking her head, she grabbed her suitcase and entered the women's room, locking the door behind her. With a sigh, she peeled off her tattered clothing, dropping it in the trash bin. Then, crossing to the mirror, she studied her image. Nothing had changed. Sydney Conner, cellist, stared back at her. Other than the sunburn and the disheveled mop of hair, she looked much the same as the woman who'd stayed at the Hotel Royale a few days before. She caught sight of her ragged fingernails and grimaced.

Though externally she could see little signs of the ordeal she'd lived through, inside, her entire world had shifted. It would take more than a simple shower to make her feel normal again.

Her thoughts wandered to Chase. He seemed to have no problem reverting to the person he'd been before the crash. But then, he didn't have a baby to worry over.

Turning the tap on full blast, she stepped into the shower, fighting the urge to hurry so she could get to the doctor. Despite her niggling worry, the soap and shampoo and hot water felt wonderful.

After toweling off, she eyed her still-flat stomach and wondered. She'd feel it if something were wrong, wouldn't she? Combing out her wet hair, she muttered a quick prayer for her unborn child, then opened her door to find Chase and the others waiting.

The sight of him, clean and in a black, Armani T-shirt and pressed khakis, made her mouth go dry. He'd shaved and tied his damp blond hair in a casual ponytail, which made him even more rakishly and elegantly handsome.

"There you are." He smiled at her, but his smile didn't touch his eyes. With a dip of his chin, he gave a signal, and the other men moved to flank them.

"Ready?"

She nodded. "I can't wait to get to a doctor."

They stepped outside into the bright sunlight and approached the limo with an almost military precision. William held the back door open. As Sydney climbed inside, Chase got in next to her. William and the other two men took the opposite seat.

The last time Sydney had ridden in a limo had been the night Reginald had broken up with her. He'd arrived for their date, flowers in hand, though this time instead of the usual red roses, he'd brought her pure white. He'd been unusually quiet, his aristocratic features reflecting his nervousness. He'd fidgeted in the plush seat, while the car took them to downtown Silverton's finest restaurant.

That night had felt mystical, magical. Sydney had actually suspected Reginald was going to propose. Instead, over aperitifs, he'd told her their relationship was over and he could no longer see her.

While the car glided silently along the curving streets, William filled them in on how they'd been located.

"The plane's emergency beacon was still working," he said. "We were surprised to learn you'd crashed on Chawder Island."

"Why?"

"You filed a flight plan to Naessa. Chawder Island is several hundred miles west of the correct route."

Chase's brows rose. "The storm must have blown Franco off course. He and Dell tried to land us safely. They were good men and damn fine pilots." He shifted restlessly. "This Chawder Island, who does it belong to?"

"The Lazlo Group is looking into that. Ownership is registered to a corporation whose existence appears to be a front for someone else."

Watching the scenery outside the car, Sydney knew a growing feeling of alarm. "This doesn't look like the road into Silverton. In fact, I'd swear we weren't even in Silvershire. Where are we?"

Chase glanced at William. The other man gave her a reassuring smile. "Carringtonshire."

Carringtonshire? That was in the northwestern part of Silvershire, a part of the country she'd never visited. The twisting road seemed to be in the remote countryside. Nothing but trees and hills could be seen, no matter how far she looked.

"Why?" She stared at William, then Chase.

William tapped his laptop case. "We're headed for the royal vacation lodge on Lake Lodan."

"Vacation lodge?" She turned on Chase. "You promised me a doctor. I want to see a doctor immediately. Before anything else, take me to a hospital."

Chase smoothed a wayward hair from her face, tucking it behind her ear. "Calm down. It's all been taken care of."

William nodded. "Yes, Miss Conner. I've taken care of everything. We should arrive at the lodge in twenty minutes, and I've arranged to have a top-notch ob-gyn meet us there."

"Top-notch?" She squinted at him suspiciously. "This Carringtonshire looks like a country area to me. How'd you manage to find a doctor like that out here in the sticks?"

"Luckily, Dr. Kallan was on holiday nearby. He's excellent." William's professional tone spoke of one used to making arrangements for others. He regarded her expectantly, making her smile faintly. If not for his beefed-up appearance, he'd be a perfect personal secretary.

She sighed. "That's a start, but honestly, I'm going to need more than just an examination. I'll need blood work and a sonogram. I need a hospital. Then I want to go home to Naessa."

William looked at Chase. So did Carlos and Jim.

"In good time, Sydney. First, we're going to Lake Lodan." Chase's cool, calculating look no longer fooled her. "After that, we'll take things one at a time."

"I don't understand." She crossed her arms. The plush

interior of the limo was starting to feel like a prison. "No more of this nonsense. Once I've seen the doctor and had my tests at a hospital, I want to go home. You can drop me at Silvershire International as soon as possible. I can arrange my own flight."

Chase's expression was closed, remote. "One step at a time, Sydney. One step at a time."

Ever-helpful William leaned forward. "Chase thought, in view of the situation, it'd be best to keep you hidden here in Carringtonshire for a little while."

"Situation? Hidden?"

The other men exchanged a look as she stared at them. Chase touched her arm. She was so angry she jerked away, glaring at him. "I think you'd better explain."

"You know someone is trying to kill you. Until we learn who and why, better safe than sorry."

She took a deep breath, letting it out slowly. "That's not your problem."

"But it is," he said smoothly. "You are carrying the prince's baby. Our employer, the Duke of Carrington, has asked us keep you safe."

"Are we back to that again? You were taking me home when—" She inhaled sharply as a horrible thought occurred to her. "You don't think the plane crash—?"

"We're looking into that, ma'am." William didn't even glance at her as he spoke. He was too preoccupied downloading information into the smallest, sleekest laptop she'd ever seen.

"If they caused the jet to crash, they killed those two pilots."

"True." Chase touched her arm lightly. "But I'm thinking hail brought it on. It was an accident."

William looked up from his screen. "Do you seriously believe that? It seems awfully convenient."

"I was there." Chase's sharp voice contained a rebuke. "Besides, no one could have known Sydney would be on that jet."

"You filed a flight plan." One of the other men spoke up, earning a sharp glance from William.

"True." Chase gave the other man a thoughtful look. "But if the jet was sabotaged, that would mean it's someone on the inside."

All three men shifted uneasily. Chase folded his arms. "Any thoughts?"

The more these men talked, the less they sounded like public relations workers. She could easily picture any of them in Silvershire's secret service.

None of the others had any answers. But they all agreed Sydney was still in grave danger.

"Right now," Chase said, his gaze intense, "whoever they are, they're probably searching frantically for you."

"Not to mention the press. They've been going wild since the princess disappeared. No one knows about the crash. We've managed to keep a lid on that." William's wry smile and quick shake of his head told her he had his doubts as to the truth of that statement.

"The press?" Sydney fought the urge to rub her aching lower back. The sooner she could talk to that doctor, the better. "Why would the press care what I do? Since they publicized Reginald's and my breakup, they've left me alone."

"You're in the news again." William swallowed, looking from her to Chase. "Reporters are scouring the streets trying to hunt you down. In the meantime, they've dug up every detail about you they could find."

"Why?" Chase's voice was cold. "Because she was Reginald's last lover before he died? I wouldn't think that's newsworthy now."

"That's only part of it. Someone leaked information to them about the pregnancy. We know it wasn't you—" he jabbed a finger in Sydney's direction "—since you were on Chawder Island when the story broke."

They all looked at Sydney.

She lifted her shoulders in a shrug. "I didn't do it. I avoid the press like the plague."

"Then who?" Chase barked, glaring at his employees. "If there's a leak at the palace, I want it found, now!"

"Understood, sir. We're looking into it."

"Who's in charge of damage control?"

William shrugged. "I'm not sure. Melody has been running the department in your absence."

"Damage control?" Sydney crossed her arms and resisted the urge to tap her feet. "Why would you even need such a thing? So I'm pregnant, and Reginald and I weren't married. Things like that happen occasionally, even in Silvershire. What's the big deal?"

"For one, you are Prince Kerwin's daughter." Chase bit out the words.

William cleared his throat, looking nervous. "There's more, and it's worse. The press is reporting you and Reginald *were* wed and that the child you carry is heir to the throne. They're citing a reliable source."

"What?" Both Chase and Sydney erupted at the same time. "It's only been four days since Reginald died."

"The papers claim you and Reginald married in a secret ceremony last month. One of them even says they have explicit photos."

Chase narrowed his gaze. "Is that so?"

Sydney gave in and rubbed her throbbing temples, then moved her hands to her lower back. "Well, they're lying. Reginald and I were never married. The only truth in all that is that I am pregnant. And—" she leaned forward, looking from one man to the other "—I really don't care what the reporters say. It doesn't matter to me. I'm pregnant, I want to rest. I just want to see a doctor and then go home."

Chase shook his head. "It's not safe."

"I don't think these people, whoever they are, will follow me back to Naessa."

"They will."

"Fine." She gave up and let herself sink back into the plush leather seat. "We'll talk about this later, after my examination."

When Chase didn't reply, she turned her attention to the scenery. Lined by granite boulders and an occasional cliff, the winding road curved through massive oaks and towering pines. Finally, Lake Lodan came into view, sunlight glinting off the water.

"It's beautiful," she said.

"The royal family's lodge is on the western side of the lake." Chase watched her intently, as though he expected her to bolt as soon as the car stopped. Not a bad idea, but hardly likely. He must have forgotten she'd seen how fast he could run.

One more sweeping curve brought them close to the lake. The wind stirred the sparkling water into choppy waves, sending them crashing against the stone cliffs. Sydney sighed, thinking of Chawder Island. Though their stay there had been brief, she'd felt as though they'd existed in another world, a cocoon filled only with her and Chase. Surreal. No wonder she felt different.

"Are we climbing?"

Chase answered with a short nod.

William looked up from his laptop. "We're nearly there."

The road became steeper. More cliffs, rocky and studded with trees, rose on one side. On the other, the lake spread out like a glistening blue jewel.

"Christ!" The driver swore. Directly ahead of them, a car swung wide around a sharp curve. Moving fast, the other driver headed directly toward them on the wrong side of the road.

"Hold on." The limo driver wrenched the wheel. The large vehicle, not made for precise turns, swung and began to skid toward the rocky cliffs. If they went over, they'd be killed.

At the last instant the other car switched lanes, again coming directly at them.

"He's trying to hit us!" William screamed, one second before the other vehicle slammed into them.

The impact spun the limo the other way. Luckily for them their rear fender barely touched the guardrail, not enough to slow their reverse sideways motion.

The other car, having hit them in the rear quarter panel, ricocheted the opposite way. It took out the guardrail, hanging on the edge for one awful moment before vanishing over the side of the cliff.

After careening left, then right, and hitting a huge boulder, the limo came to a stop. They all looked at each other. Chase held Sydney in place, while the other men shot out of the car, guns drawn.

"All clear," William said.

"Come on." Chase got out first, extending his hand to Sydney. Shakily, she climbed from the backseat.

"That was no random accident," Chase shook his head, his expression grim. "I'm thinking that was another attempt to take you out of the picture."

"No way," she scoffed. "It had to be an accident, a drunk driver or something. First off, how would they even know where we are? Second, I still don't know why anyone would want to kill me."

"You're carrying the prince's only child." He caught her arm. "That might be reason enough for some people."

William and the other two men peered over the rail. The limo driver was on his cell phone, no doubt calling in the accident.

"I want to see." Sydney shook off his hand and went to the edge of the cliff. The other car had come to rest at the bottom of the rock wall, a crumpled heap of twisted metal. "I hope you called for an ambulance," she told William.

"I called the police. They'll dispatch medical assistance."

"If they survived." Again, Chase spoke almost in her ear. Still dazed, Sydney fought the urge to turn her face into his chest for comfort.

Looking shaken, their driver walked over. His short, black hair was mussed, as if he'd run his fingers through it in agitation. His face drained of color, he shook his head. "They were either drunk or…"

"Something," Chase put in smoothly. The warning look he gave Sydney let her know he didn't want his speculation about the near miss revealed to the driver, a man not in his employ.

Lights flashing, the police arrived, along with a fire truck and an ambulance. Because of the wreck's location, only one police cruiser stayed to take the report; the others drove back the way they'd come. There was a public swimming area further north that would give them access to the crash if they drove up the beach.

Once they'd finished supplying the remaining officer with details, and determined the limousine was still drivable, they climbed back in to resume their journey.

A few more miles and several more curves in the road later, they pulled up to massive iron gates. Worked into the iron was the royal coat of arms. She sighed, watching as the gates swung slowly open. The Royal Family of Silvershire's private lake lodge, one of their many vacation hideaways. This particular one she'd never heard of, though the press had reported on many others. In such a remote location, with no easy access, it seemed even the press hadn't been able to infiltrate these gated walls. No doubt this was why Chase had chosen it as a hiding place for her.

After the accident that might not have been an accident, she was beginning to think Chase wasn't so far from the mark. Until those crazy people were caught, maybe staying here with protection was the best option.

Inhaling deeply, still shaky, she tried for calm. None of their party had been hurt, but if the other car had merely made a blunder, she felt horrible for them.

"Chase?"

He looked at her, his hazel eyes serious. "Yes?"

"Can we call and check on those people back there? You know, whether they lived or…"

"Died? We can check with the police department later." His serious expression told her he was just as affected by what had happened as she.

"Miss Conner?" William leaned forward. "I think you'll

like it here. The royal family maintains a very sumptuous lifestyle, even at this lake lodge. We have a full-service salon, a masseuse and personal trainer, as well as a fully equipped gym and indoor pool." He smiled, too brightly, as though he was trying to erase the last hour with his words. "What more could you ask for?"

What more indeed? A clean bill of health for the baby.

She turned to look at Chase, startled to find him watching her intently.

"What?" She asked.

He shook his head and looked away without answering.

As the limo drove through, the gates closed behind them with a clank. Sydney let her head sink back against the plush leather and briefly closed her eyes. Deciding to stay was a relief of sorts. She was exhausted and could use a few days of rest and relaxation, especially in such lavish surroundings. No doubt this place had the kind of luxury she rarely got to enjoy anymore, especially when traveling with the symphony.

But she couldn't relax until she'd received a clean bill of health both for herself and for her baby. She sat up, eager to see the physician and begin the tests which would, she hoped, relieve all her worries.

William stowed his laptop and the two other men put away their Palm Pilots. Briefly, she considered asking if the royal PR department issued the devices as standard equipment. Then she caught sight of the "lodge" and forgot all that.

Perched on the cliff like some massive cedar hawk overlooking the lake, the building looked large enough to easily accommodate one hundred or more guests. Through the two-story window over the door, she could see a wall of windows on the waterside, filling the house with light and a breathtaking view.

The limo coasted to a stop. The driver got out and opened the door for Sydney. When she stepped into the blinding sunlight, she stumbled. Instantly, Chase was there, offering his arm.

At first, she wanted to snub him, to show him she was perfectly capable of walking in on her own. But when she saw the massive double doors open and a footman wearing royal livery emerge, she changed her mind.

Though she might carry the blood of a princess, and, as a child, had often longed to meet her sire, Reginald had been her only exposure to royalty. Quite frankly, she found the prospect intimidating.

"Come on." Keeping her arm in his, Chase led her up the stone steps, through the great doors and into the foyer. Their footsteps echoed on the green marble floor.

He released her arm as the doors closed behind them. Turning slowly, Sydney tried to take it all in, but couldn't.

Gleaming floors, walls and ceiling crafted of warm oak, she had an impression of granite and wood and steel, skill-fully melded into a welcoming warmth that could have won design awards. This place was the stuff of glossy magazines, reminding her of her mother's penthouse condo.

As she took it all in, she spied a familiar black instrument case leaning against one wall.

"My cello!" She crossed the room, trailing her fingers over the black case reverently. "How did you locate it?"

"We had it flown in." William smiled as both she and Chase turned to stare at him in surprise. "Rest assured, it wasn't damaged in the shooting. The hotel was holding it in their lost-and-found department, along with your suitcase full of clothing. We've put that in your room."

Chase shot her a look that said I told you so.

No matter. Sydney sighed with pleasure. Now all she needed was a clean bill of health for her baby and a way home. Then her life would be just about perfect. Even if her baby would never have a father.

A man who could have only been the butler cleared his throat. "May I show you to your room?"

She swung round to eye Chase. "I'd prefer to see the doctor first."

"Get settled and freshen up." Despite his size, or maybe because of it, Chase looked at home in the deliberately rugged yet opulent surroundings. He stood out from the other men like a rare coin among wooden currency. "I'll send someone for you when the doctor is ready."

Nodding, she turned to follow the butler and realized her misgivings were because she didn't want to leave Chase—proving once again that she wasn't herself since the plane crash. Despite feeling mortified, she couldn't stop herself from looking at him over her shoulder.

"You'll be fine." The kindness in his voice told her that somehow he must have understood.

Her room was, like the rest of the lodge, luxuriously comfortable. Everything, from the oversized bed covered with a cream-colored, exquisitely soft, down comforter, to the well-made, gleaming oak furniture, was of the highest quality. The room had the feel of an ultraprivate, ultraluxurious, resort for the very pampered ultrarich.

Feet sinking into the thick carpet, Sydney padded over to the windows and pulled the heavy lined drapes open.

She gasped out loud at the view. Her room overlooked the lake. It spread out below her like a liquid sapphire, shimmering in the sunlight. Whitecap waves dotted the surface, along with sailboats and the occasional yacht. She could make out other homes dotting the countryside, all large and luxurious, though none matched this one for sheer magnificence.

Since she'd showered earlier, she had nothing to do but wait.

"The doctor's here."

Startled, Sydney turned to find a smiling young woman in a maid's uniform hovering in the doorway. Evidently, she'd once again forgotten to close her door.

"If you'll follow me, please?"

Eagerness warring with nervousness, Sydney went.

Chapter 8

Once the examination was complete, Sydney waited, her heartbeat booming in her ears. Dr. Kallan had confirmed Sydney's suspicion that only an ultrasound examination and a complete blood workup would tell if her baby was all right. The equipment to do this test was, of course, only available at a hospital. The nearest facility was in the next town inland, a good thirty-minute drive on winding roads. Dr. Kallan had gone to tell Chase and the others.

A moment later, the doctor returned. He smiled reassuringly as he patted Sydney's hand. "They've agreed to take you into town. The car is being brought around now. I'll meet you at the emergency room there."

A grim-faced Chase and his three stooges waited for her in the great room.

"Ready?" His cool gaze gave away nothing.

Schooling her own expression to match his, Sydney nodded.

Though they left by unmarked car, someone must have tipped off the reporters. When their black Mercedes pulled up to the emergency-room entrance, a cluster of photographers eagerly awaited their arrival.

"Keep driving," Chase instructed the driver. "This isn't an emergency. Go around to the back."

"They've probably got people stationed there, as well." Sydney kept her tone calm. "If so, take me back to the emergency room. Dr. Kallan said he'd be waiting for me there."

"It doesn't look like we're going to be able to avoid the reporters." William sounded energized.

"I'll be fine." Sydney sighed. "I've been dealing with them off and on for most of my life."

"Don't speak to the press." Chase met her gaze. "Let us handle them."

"Don't worry. I have nothing to say to them."

Scowling, he glared at her. "They think you married the prince."

"I know."

"Wishing it was true?"

She only shrugged off his sharp-edged question. At least if she had, her baby would be acknowledged. Legitimate.

On the other hand, her child would be heir to the throne. He or she would never have a normal life. Thinking of her half-brothers and -sisters and the rarefied air they lived in, she'd already decided she didn't want that for her own child, not if she could help it. She'd planned to discuss alternatives with Reginald.

But since he'd refused even to speak to her, that talk

had never happened. Now it was all up to her to take care of her baby.

Chase eyed her, his sharp gaze missing nothing. "I've got people setting up an official press conference for you this afternoon, so you can set the record straight. Once it's known you're not carrying the next official heir, maybe the death threats will cease."

She sighed. "I was hoping hiding out here would take care of that."

"Until we know more about that car that tried to run us off the road, I'm taking no chances. Plus, with all the reporters here," he gestured at the waiting crowd, "whoever is after you will know exactly where you are."

She peered through the tinted glass, eyeing the eager faces, the microphones and cameras. Somehow, without intending to, she'd managed to achieve what her mother had always craved. She was in the spotlight.

All Sydney wanted to do was return home to Naessa and her life of relative anonymity. She wanted to lick her wounds in private and prepare for the upcoming birth of her child.

"Coming here might have been a big mistake." William leaned forward. "They'll make the connection between this town and the royal lodge. Before long they'll be camped outside the gates."

"I needed to have tests run." Sydney kept her tone firm. "So I had to come here whether you like it or not. Plus, you can't keep me hidden forever." Unbidden, thoughts of Chawder Island intruded. She couldn't help but speculate on what would have happened if they'd stayed longer. She'd never experienced anything quite like the explosiveness of nearly making love with Chase. She wondered what the real thing would be like.

The heat in Chase's gaze told her he shared her thoughts.

Embarrassed, she looked away, back out her window to where the vultures circled with their flashbulbs and their video cameras.

The car slowly circled the building. Clusters of reporters were gathered around each entrance.

"They're unbelievable." Sydney had gotten her first experience with paparazzi early. As a young girl, her mother had enjoyed taking her out in public dressed in outlandishly expensive outfits. Someone had always been around to snap a picture of the illegitimate princess and her lovely mother for the tabloids.

Her mother had considered it amusing. She'd preened for the cameras, thriving on the notoriety. Sydney had always been the opposite. As she'd grown, she'd begun to see the press as stalkers and her mother as a panderer.

Once grown, she'd done her best to live in a way designed not to draw attention. The more quietly she lived her life, the less the press hounded her. Lack of flash and bling made for boring pictures. Soon, the press all but ignored her. A cello-playing, illegitimate princess who never partied wasn't considered newsworthy.

Until the Crown Prince of Silvershire had taken a shine to her. Dating Reginald had changed all that. She grimaced at the thought. Like her mother, the prince had seemed to enjoy the attention. Sydney had been content to leave him the limelight. She'd preferred to remain in the shadows.

Damned if she was going to let them hound her baby.

"Take us back to the emergency room," Chase ordered the driver. "Pull up as close to the door as possible. I'll take her in there."

The instant she and Chase stepped from the car, they were surrounded. Flashbulbs popped and microphones were thrust in her face while the reporters shouted questions. Stone-faced, Chase shouldered his way through while Sydney clung to his back.

Each time someone shoved a mike in front of him, he repeated four words. "Press conference later today."

Once inside, they found the brazen press had followed.

"There." Chase pointed. A nurse held a door open for them, letting them bypass the check-in desk. One of the perks of being attached to royalty, Sydney supposed.

"Wait here." Her shoes squeaking on the linoleum, the nurse indicated two hard plastic chairs. "Dr. Kallan is on his way."

Sydney sat. Chase remained standing, his hands crammed in his pockets.

"What's wrong?" she asked softly.

Instead of answering, he responded with a question. "You really don't like the spotlight, do you?"

So that was it. Of course. He was head of public relations. Dealing with reporters was his job and, she suspected, his life.

"I told you I didn't. Why? Was there something wrong with the way I avoided them?"

Though she'd meant the question as sort of a joke, he regarded her with a serious expression. "Do you really want the picture they splash all over the newspapers to be one of you with your face burrowed into my chest?"

She shrugged. "Honestly, I don't really care. All I was thinking about at the time was getting through the crowd, not how I'd look in the news."

"But—"

"Miss Conner?" The nurse was back. "If you'll follow me."

Chase started to rise, too, but Sydney stopped him with a look. "You can wait here."

The muscle that worked in his jaw was the only sign he gave of how he felt about her request. But he did as she'd asked. As the automatic doors closed behind her, Sydney felt a stab of regret, which she automatically suppressed. Her baby's welfare had nothing to do with Chase and wanting his support was only more foolishness on her part. Plus, all the water she'd had to drink in preparation made her uncomfortable.

The sonogram was done with quiet efficiency, the warmed gel and the gentle motions of the technician soothing. After they'd finished and cleaned her up, she was taken to another room where a different nurse drew blood.

Barely forty-five minutes had passed before Sydney rejoined Chase in the private waiting room.

"All done?" Chase's hooded gaze spoke of a simmering anger. Since he had no reason to be angry, Sydney pretended not to notice.

"It'll be a little while until I get the results." Despite her best efforts to sound cool, calm and collected, her voice caught.

"Don't worry." He touched her arm. "Everything will be all right." He held her gaze for the space of a heartbeat before he looked away.

Because she hoped he was right, she said nothing. Instead, she studied his chiseled profile. Perversely, she wished he wasn't so damn beautiful. If he weren't, she might find it easier to hate him, if it came to that when all this ended.

She could deal with that, she told herself, as long as she

didn't lose her heart. And God knew, she would never be that foolish again.

The nurse emerged, causing them both to look up. "If you'll follow me?"

This time, when Chase followed, Sydney let him.

They were led down a long hall to a small office. Two high-backed leather chairs faced a mahogany desk.

"The doctor will be with you shortly," the nurse said.

Sydney stared at the chair, her rapid heartbeat feeling as though it were in her throat.

"Sit."

"I don't know if I can."

His smile was a flash of white. "Of course you can. What else are you going to do? You can't pace in such a tiny room."

He had a point. Sydney sat.

When he lowered himself into the chair next to her and then took her hand, she froze. He squeezed her fingers and she decided to take the comfort he offered.

A moment later, Dr. Kallan bustled into the room, smiling broadly. "I have good news. You're absolutely fine and your baby is developing normally."

Sydney released her breath. Clutching Chase's hand, she turned to him, her eyes filling. "Thank God."

Chase's hard expression softened. "Congratulations."

Impulsively, she leaned over and kissed him before jumping to her feet and hugging the doctor. "You don't know what a relief it is to hear that."

The gray-haired doctor smiled back. "You're about eight weeks along. Everything looks good."

"Could you tell the baby's sex from this sonogram?"

He shook his head. "Not yet. It's too early. We can

usually determine the sex of the fetus accurately by sixteen to eighteen weeks using ultrasound or fifteen to sixteen weeks with an amniocentesis. Or, if you'd like to come back in two weeks, we can do a CVS, chorionic villus sampling. That's usually reliable at ten or eleven weeks."

"I won't be here then."

At her words, Chase stiffened.

The doctor smiled. "Then I'm afraid you'll have to guess a bit longer." He stood and held out his hand.

After she shook it, he inclined his head. "If you need anything else, have your people give me a call."

Once in the hallway, Sydney headed for the doors under the sign marked Exit. Chase stopped her.

"We need to discuss a strategy."

"A strategy for what?"

"Dealing with the press."

She sighed. "What's to discuss? We'll just do the same thing we did before. Breeze through them with a bunch of 'No comments.'"

"We can't. We can get away with ignoring them once. If we do it twice, they'll speculate."

"So? Let them." She tried to pull away, but his hand on her shoulder prevented her. "Let me go."

"Do you want to read a story in the morning about how you got rid of your baby?"

Shocked, she stared up at him. "What do you mean?"

"You know how some of them can be, especially the tabloids. Lacking truth to report, they'll simply make something up."

"I would never do such a thing."

"They don't know that. The general public doesn't either."

"You can tell you're in public relations." She couldn't keep the bitterness from her voice.

Stoically, he watched her.

"Fine. We'll make a statement. What do you want me to say?" Despite her anger, her emotions were perilously close to the surface. The back of her throat stung, and she blinked away tears.

"Sydney—" With a curse, he crushed her to him, covering her mouth with his in a hard, possessive kiss.

Neither heard the doors silently swing open.

A flashbulb popped. Then another. Suddenly, reporters with camcorders and cameras surrounded them.

Jaw clenched tightly, Chase released her.

She turned in time to see the cameraman flash a thumbs-up sign. She recognized the reporter standing next to him as Chris Endov, one of the beat reporters for the *Daily Press,* Silvershire's main paper.

"What do you want, Endov?" Chase asked. Though he sounded pleasant enough, Sydney recognized the thread of steel underlying his tone.

"I have a few questions." Endov came closer. "For you, Miss Conner. First you're hot and heavy with the prince, and now that he's dead, you're with his royal publicist? Any particular reason for that?"

Chase answered before Sydney could even open her mouth. "No comment." Arm around her waist, he began shepherding her away.

The reporters followed, shouting questions.

"Are you still pregnant?"

Sydney tensed. Without even looking at them, Chase tossed off a quick, "No comment."

"No, wait." Sydney stopped, turning to face the restless

throng. "I want to answer that. Yes, I definitely am still pregnant. I came here to have a routine checkup."

More flashbulbs. Several of the camcorders were rolling. Sydney tried to look a dignified as possible, memories of her mother's simpering pandering haunting her.

"Do you know your baby's sex?" someone shouted.

She forced a smile. "No, it's too early for that."

"Were you and Prince Reginald secretly married?"

Without waiting for her answer, another reporter followed up. "Now that the prince is dead, are you planning to step forward and proclaim your unborn child heir to the throne?"

She stood straight and tall, the afternoon breeze lifting her hair. "Absolutely not."

"Then," someone else called out, "you're saying your baby will be born unwanted and illegitimate, like you?"

Someone gasped. The rowdy reporters fell silent, one by one. Chase cursed.

For Sydney, time seemed to stand still. She blanched, turning her face away from the crowd, toward Chase, longing for the comfort of his broad chest.

He took a step toward her and stopped, his expression dark. When she raised her gaze to him, she knew she wasn't strong enough or quick enough to hide her stark pain.

"Old wound," she said, striving for lightness but sounding instead as though she'd taken a blow to the solar plexus. She kept her eyes fixed on Chase while she spoke, using him as an anchor.

Something dark, something haunted, crossed his face. She noticed how he fisted his hands, though he kept them at his sides while he searched the crowd to try and find out who'd spoken.

She didn't want to know.

Someone cleared their throat.

"Who asked that?" Voice deadly calm, Chase searched their faces. No one stepped forward.

"Then we're done here," he said, taking Sydney's arm to lead her off.

"I have one more question." A woman wearing too much makeup and an overloud orange dress raised her hand.

Chase sighed. "Go ahead."

"Miss Conner, you never answered the question." Her broad face had the determination of a bulldog. "Is there any truth to the rumor that you and Prince Reginald were married before his death?"

His expression furious, Chase shook his head.

"She's engaged to me," he said.

Several in the crowd gasped audibly, but none louder than Sydney.

Once said, Chase wanted to call those words back. He had no idea what had come over him. The declaration had just popped out. From nowhere. He knew better. What he'd said was not only foolish, but improbable, implausible and highly suspect. Yet now, having said them, he realized he'd have to make them work—somehow, until something could be done to rectify his mistake.

Sydney gazed up at him, her eyes wide and impossibly blue. "Engaged? We are so not—"

"Talking about this now," Chase put in smoothly. Then, partly because she had a mutinous set to her chin, and partly because her open mouth just looked so damn inviting, he kissed her again.

As before, the moment his mouth covered hers, he was lost in a tidal wave of desire and need. Standing stiffly, she sighed into his mouth. Then, as lust all but consumed him, she brought her arms up around his neck, tangled her free hand in his hair, and held him in place. Her tongue stroked and tempted and teased and either she was the best damn actress he'd ever met, or she craved him as badly as he wanted her.

He almost forgot they were standing in a hospital surrounded by reporters. His desire for Sydney filled him, and any other time, any other place, they would have made hot, urgent love.

Out of the question. He lifted his head, breathing raggedly, and fought to regain his shattered control.

Now though, the ultimate PR professional had a pressing problem. With her wild kisses and her body melded so close to his, she'd aroused the hell out of him. They had a crowd of spectators. If he turned to face the reporters now, they'd know exactly how much he wanted Sydney, his brand new fiancée.

Her breathing as ragged as his, she hid her face against his chest, her color high.

The reporters all shouted questions—and ribald comments—at once. Dimly he became aware of flashbulbs popping. Damn. He had to hand it to her. Sydney had succeeded in making him do what he'd never done in his entire career in public relations—lose control in front of the press. *Hell,* he thought ruefully, hanging on to the last shreds of his tattered restraint as he eyed the news cameras, in this case, *in front of the entire world.*

Still, he couldn't help longing to finish what he'd inadvertently started. *Another time, another place…*

Regretfully, he took a deep breath and, keeping Sydney tight against him, turned partially to face them. Ignoring the upraised hands, the videocams, the shouts, he forced his expression into an indulgent smile. "Ladies, gentlemen. May we have a little privacy, please?" A foolish request. He knew it, they knew it, but by simply asking, he'd guaranteed himself a bit more time to get his unruly hormones under control.

As he'd expected, this caused a good-natured uproar. Most laughed and shouted ribald jokes. A few loudly protested. While they argued among themselves, Chase tried to think of playing golf, which was the most calming, unsexy thing he could think of.

He had to give Sydney credit. Though one look at her dilated pupils and unsteady breathing told him she was just as affected as he, she smoothed her hair with one hand, her shirt with the other, and straightened. When she did look toward the crowd, her serene expression gave nothing away.

She wore, he thought with grudging respect, the face of someone used to dealing with the press. In his line of work, he had to admire that. Royals like her made his job that much easier.

Together they ignored the reporters. Thirty seconds later, feeling almost normal, he removed his arm from Sydney's shoulders.

"So are you aiming to move up in the palace hierarchy, Mr. Savage?"

He answered smoothly, though he knew what they meant. "Not possible. I don't have royal blood. You should know better than that."

"But she does." A woman with short dark hair, dressed casually in faded jeans and hiking boots, pointed at Sydney. "She's a princess of Naessa. What does this bode for the two countries' continued relations?"

Political implications. Not good. Carrington hadn't briefed him on the official palace response.

While he searched for a suitable nonanswer, Sydney straightened and lifted her chin. With his hand still on her shoulder, he could feel her tension—she all but vibrated with it.

Her blue eyes were cool as she measured the other woman. "No, as someone else so succinctly pointed out earlier, I'm illegitimate. I have no real title. I'm certain there are quite a few of Prince Kerwin's by-blows running around Naessa. My actions carry neither political clout nor connotations."

This brought another round of shouted queries.

Sydney held up her hand. "You know and I know that I have no real claim to fame. I live a quiet life, not bothering anyone. And no one, including the press, bothers me. Most importantly, I don't think any of this makes me particularly newsworthy."

"You were seen quite frequently with Prince Reginald, before he died."

She sighed. "He was a great fan of the symphony."

The dryness of her tone made a few of them chuckle.

"Were you two lovers while she was sleeping with the Prince?" Paul Seacrist, of *Silvershire Inquisitor* fame, stepped forward. The tabloid, known as *The Quiz,* bore the logo of a large, all-seeing eye. Which often felt particularly appropriate, since their cameramen seemed to be everywhere.

Sydney gasped. Chase squeezed her shoulder, letting her know he intended to handle this one himself.

At the smug knowing leer on the man's pinched face, a stab of anger went through Chase, sharp as a knife. If he gave in to impulse and punched the guy out, there'd be hell to pay. What a field day they'd have with that!

He took a deep breath. He hadn't gotten to his position as head of PR by losing control.

Quieting, all the reporters watched them, waiting for a reaction, cameras ready.

Suddenly, Chase realized he recognized the voice. It had been Seacrist who earlier had hurt Sydney by calling her illegitimate and unwanted. He took a step forward.

Seacrist continued to wait expectantly. Something in his expression told Chase he knew if Chase touched him, not only would he have the story of the year, but a million-dollar lawsuit, as well.

Damn it!

It took all of his training and skill, but Chase kept his head. "You've just insulted me, Miss Conner and the deceased prince. I expect an apology. Now."

"Apology?" The other man looked disappointed. "I was only asking a simple question. I meant no insult."

Chase inclined his head, accepting the reporter's words, since he could do little else.

There were more questions, all routine. Chase fielded two or three about the baby, answering in such generalities that he told them absolutely nothing. He'd developed a knack for this sort of thing, appearing to be utterly forthright while revealing little of the truth.

Doing what he was paid to do, he should be in his element. But he was not. For the first time in his career, Chase felt as if he were watching the reporters who vied for his attention from a distance. Instead of feeling energized, he felt annoyed and irritated.

Through all this, Sydney held herself regally, gazing at

the reporters defiantly. Her cinnamon hair glowed, even in the harsh, artificial light, and her eyes stood out starkly in her pale, pale face. While trying to hide her hurt, she was absolutely beautiful. Watching her, he felt a clenching low in his stomach.

God help him, he still longed for her. Even now, he wanted to kiss the side of her long, creamy throat, tangle his hands in her lustrous hair. Instead, he leaned closer, inhaling her scent, and whispered in her ear. "Are you ready?"

"For what?" she mouthed.

"To make a run for it. After all we've given them, we should be home free."

She rolled her eyes. "Do you really think they'll let us go?"

"That's why we're going to make a run for it. We'll leave them no choice."

She nodded. "Then let's go. But this time, I'm going first." Taking a deep breath, she plunged through the crowd for the doorway. Amused, he followed.

Like sharks moving in for the kill, the press surrounded her, blocking her path, still calling out questions.

Undeterred, she continued to push forward.

Following behind her, Chase gave them all a rueful smile. "What, no privacy?"

The ones closest to him laughed.

Finally, they reached the exit and squeezed through the doors, heading for the car. Once he'd seen Sydney safely inside he turned to face the reporters, one hand on the door handle.

"Come on, people. Settle down." He heaved a loud, mock sigh, and waited. Once they'd quieted, he gave them an impersonal smile. "I'd planned to hold a press conference later, but now I see no need. You have had more information than I ever intended you to have."

There were several collective groans. Finally, he held up his hand, and they quieted. "I think that's all, folks. We just gave you all a fantastic story, announcing our engagement. So it seems to me you'd take that and run with it and allow us some small measure of privacy. We'd like to celebrate— just not in front of a crowd."

This time, he spoke a partial truth. He wanted to be alone with Sydney, to explain why he'd said what he had.

One last, diehard newshound stepped forward. "What about the baby? How does it make you feel, Mr. Savage, knowing your wife-to-be is pregnant with another man's child? Not just any other man, but Prince Reginald, your boss?"

Even the casual mention of Reginald in the same context as Sydney grated on Chase's nerves. And the reminder she was pregnant by another man was much-needed. It served to remind him why he couldn't allow his desire for her to cloud his judgment any further. Put that way, his sudden urge to help Sydney seemed stupid—something he already knew.

Not since he'd been left at the altar by Kayla, then publicly humiliated by her announcement that the baby he'd thought was his belonged to another man, had he allowed his emotions to rule him. His attempt to take some of the heat off her had just guaranteed that the press would continue to speculate. And to hound them.

Chapter 9

William and the others regarded them curiously as they got settled. Sydney didn't speak, not even after Chase had climbed in beside her and pulled the door closed behind him. She waited until the car pulled out and the other men were once again involved with their electronic gadgets.

"Chase?"

With an effort, he made himself look at her, steeling himself for what he knew was to come. Based on his experience with other women, he expected theatrics, shouting and tears and possibly even curses.

He'd forgotten he was dealing with a princess by blood, even if she didn't carry the official title.

Her regal bearing and the simmering anger in her husky voice were the only signs she was upset.

And all he could think about was how badly he wanted to kiss her again.

Leaning forward, she looked him in the eye. "What exactly happened back there?"

Feeling reckless, Chase let a slow smile spread across his face. "I think we just got engaged."

William looked up so sharply he nearly popped his neck. One of the other men dropped his Palm Pilot, fumbling, his seat belt still clasped, to retrieve it.

"What was that? What did you say?"

"I said that Miss Conner and I have just become engaged."

"You're kidding!" William exploded. "There's no way—"

Maybe because his raw emotions simmered too close to the surface for him to control, Chase felt his cool facade slip. He let it show in his eyes as he looked at the other man. "Why is that, William?"

Taking the hint, William closed his mouth and sat back in his seat. He grabbed his own Palm Pilot and began fumbling with it. "Never mind," he mumbled. "Don't know what I was thinking. Congratulations, sir. Ma'am."

Sydney made a rude sound, causing William to raise his head in surprise. A sharp glare from Chase made him look away again.

"Well?"

He looked down into her upturned face and sighed. Even after all that, after knowing he'd messed up big-time and would have to find a way to correct it, he wanted to kiss her. "Can we talk about this later?" he grumbled.

She glanced at the others, trying to pretend not to listen and doing a poor job of it, and sighed. "Certainly. Though it will be at my convenience, not yours. Agreed?"

"Agreed."

When she looked away, Chase set his jaw and stared

straight ahead. He could feel Sydney's resentment, and he couldn't really blame her. Aware the others were sneaking quick glances at him, he ignored them, hyperaware of the press of her thigh against his. He couldn't help but wonder what it was about Sydney, how even now his desire for her was such that all he could think about was pulling her onto his lap and kissing her thoroughly.

He shifted in the seat, trying to make space where there was none. Since he wasn't able to do so, Sydney took care of the problem for him. Scrunching up so close to the door she must have been uncomfortable, she moved so that no part of her body touched him. At all.

He felt this absence of touch a thousand times more sharply than he should have.

When they pulled up to the royal lodge, everyone scrambled to exit the car. Except Sydney. Shoulders stiff, she climbed out and shot him a look over her shoulder. Her eyes the color of a storm-tossed sea, she shook her head. By the time he recovered enough to go after her, she'd disappeared into the house.

Practically running, Sydney barreled up the stairs and turned right when she should have turned left. The hallway looked the same, but she found herself in a large library instead of the bedroom she'd been assigned.

Curious, she eyed the floor-to-ceiling bookshelves with a dawning sense of wonder. Inspecting a shelf, then another, she saw classics and current bestsellers, research material and picture books. Whoever had collected these books had been a person of vast and varying interests.

So engrossed was she in taking in this smorgasbord of

reading material, she nearly missed the huge portrait of Reginald hanging over the antique writing desk.

Her breath caught. Feet sinking in the plush carpet, she moved slowly closer, taking in his blond hair and blue eyes. Would her child look like this, or would there be a combination of both their features, hair color and eyes?

The father of her baby. Crown Prince Reginald, now dead. Studying his patrician features, she waited for the familiar anguished feeling, but felt nothing but a sort of distant sorrow.

"Missing your lover?" Chase's voice, harsh and low, sent shivers of warning along her spine.

She didn't answer; instead she continued to examine the portrait. Remarkably lifelike—and life-sized—the painting had to have been made fairly recently.

Chase moved to stand beside her. "Cold-looking bastard, wasn't he?"

With a gasp, she turned to face him. Contempt and an icy sort of rage filled his face. But he was looking at the painting, not at her.

"Chase," she began.

"I know. I shouldn't speak ill of the dead."

With a nod, she turned to go, her heart heavy.

"Sydney…" The anguish in his deep voice stopped her, made her turn to face him.

"What was he to you?" He jabbed his finger toward the portrait. "I can't reconcile the idea of you with him."

"I thought he loved me."

He looked at her, hunger blazing from his eyes, but did not touch her. "And you," he asked. "Did you love him back?"

Feeling as though she was suffocating, she stepped back, away from the man who'd inexplicably made her realize what she'd felt for Reginald hadn't been love. Not by a long shot. "I thought I did." She choked out her reply and then, because she was afraid of what else she might say, brushed past him and out the door. Hoping she could remember the way to her room, she made her way down the hallway, telling herself she was glad when he didn't follow.

Though she wanted an explanation for his bizarre announcement, that'd have to wait until later. Right now, her emotions were too raw, her feelings about him too conflicted. What he'd told the press at the hospital had shocked her. She didn't know if Chase really thought he was helping her by announcing a fictitious engagement, or if he was mocking her.

Or, she sighed as a third possibility occurred to her, he might be trying yet another ploy to get her to remain at Lake Lodan.

Quite honestly, she didn't know what to think, how to feel, where to go. The only thing she knew for certain was she needed time to figure things out.

What was wrong with her? Covering her face with her hands, she couldn't decide whether to laugh or cry.

She'd come to crave Chase Savage. When he entered the room, everyone else ceased to exist. When he moved, the masculine grace of his muscular body made her catch her breath. One look from him and her throat went dry.

And the explosive passion when they touched haunted her dreams. His kisses, his touch, the way his hard body felt under her exploring fingers, made her quiver. Even now.

She'd begun to wonder how colorless her life would seem once Chase was no longer part of it. Such an admission, even to herself, shook her to the core.

Knowing her hormones were out of whack due to her pregnancy didn't help either. She could only blame hormones for so much emotional upheaval.

The only thing she knew for certain was when he kissed her, she forgot all reason. Merely seeing his hard profile made her long to soften his expression with kisses.

Something in him called to her. If she'd met him before Reginald, before she carried another man's child, she might have taken a chance on him.

Now, she couldn't afford to take a chance on anything.

She located her room without further incident. Once inside, she changed into a comfortable pair of jeans and sneakers. She felt confined, trapped in a twenty-five-thousand-square-foot mansion with iron gates on one side and cliffs and a lake on the other.

Then she spied her cello. With a relieved sigh, she lifted the case and headed back for the library, praying she didn't run into Chase. With its rich oak floors, walls and ceilings, the acoustics should be wonderful. She padded down the hall, trying to fill her mind with the notes she'd play.

The cello had always been her salvation in the past. It would save her now, as well. She'd lose herself in the music and forget all about her problems, even if her solution was only temporary.

Once she reached her destination, she grabbed a comfortable, French-style chair and began setting up her instrument.

Reverently, she popped open the case. Unharmed, the maple gleamed as softly as if she'd just polished it. Lovingly, she removed the cello and, holding the neck lightly with one hand, she reached for the bow. She was startled to notice her fingers shook.

This bow, despite its origins, was her favorite bow ever. Reginald had ordered it custom-made for her. He'd allowed her to choose her own horsehair and she'd selected the finest, whitest hair herself. Some cellists preferred a darker hair, believing it "grabbed" better, but she liked her bow to glide across the strings. She preferred a clean, pure sound.

Once she had everything ready, she gave the cello one final check and began to play.

After Sydney had left, Chase had studied the portrait of the man who now felt like an enemy, and wondered. What had Sydney seen in the man? His features reflected his arrogance, his disdain for anything not directed at him, his comfort, his pleasure. Reginald had been dissolute, a player and a wastrel. Seeing Sydney mooning over his likeness had made fury twist in Chase's gut.

He didn't want to try and analyze the reasons for this, so he'd left the library and stormed off to his own room, glad it was far from hers.

Once there, he'd dropped onto the bed and tried to call Carrington on the new cell phone William had given him. When he'd reached the duke's voice mail, he'd left a message, planning to ask for a reassignment back in Silverton. Then, in urgent need of distraction, he'd just decided to wander downstairs to the great room and indulge in some hundred-year-old Scotch, when he heard an unusual noise.

A note.

The sound was haunting, like ghosts teasing the wind. Chase listened, not sure what he was hearing, only knowing it was a different kind of music than he'd ever heard before.

Skittering across his skin, the sound teased, taunted. Led him to take a step forward, feeling as though he'd been bewitched by some ancient spell.

He went looking for the source of the sound, knowing it could be only one thing. At the door to the library he paused, listening as his amazement grew. He'd known she was talented, but classical music had never been his thing. Until now.

Then he saw her, red hair ablaze in the muted light. Sydney. Her music called to him, true. But *she* called to him even more.

Transfixed, he stood, and watched her play.

The polished maple of her cello glowed softly. Eyes closed, she appeared lost in coaxing the sound from her instrument. Oblivious to him or anyone else, her elegant hand led her bow across the strings in swift, yet sensuous gliding. Rapid, then slow, each sweep brought forth a haunting sound, as though the cello wept.

This music was as different from classic rock as day was from night. Normally, not at all his cup of tea.

But somehow, he was charmed. Enthralled. He longed to touch her, to kiss her pulse where it jumped at the hollow of her throat. Instead, he stood in the shadows and listened and watched.

The notes glided and climbed. The tempo grew faster. Sydney's bow flew, her face flushed, eyes still closed.

When the last note died off, she opened her eyes in a sudden flash of blue.

His heart caught in his chest.

Desire clawed at him. Lust and need and yearning propelled him toward her without even thinking.

He wanted her. Now.

Gaze still locked with his, she hurriedly set the cello and bow aside, and lifted herself up to meet him halfway. His hard, fierce kiss swallowed her soft cry.

Finally, Chase let himself do what he'd longed to do each and every time he saw her. Feeling as if he were a blind man who'd thus far been denied the power of touch, he drew his hands over her, savoring each lush curve, each satin hollow, memorizing her shape and scent and feel.

Body arching toward his hands, she matched the urgency of his caresses with her own. Her long, elegant fingers stroked him, until he was shaking with a need so intense he felt violent.

Their clothing was an unwanted barrier for each of them.

"The door," she managed, no doubt fearing a servant would wander in.

He crossed to the doorway and with one swift motion, tugged the door closed. Then, impatient for her once more, he returned and kissed her. The long, sensual kiss had them both breathing hard.

Shaking, he managed to undo the buttons of her blouse without tearing it. She tried to do the same to his shirt and could not. When she looked at him, her eyes wild and so dark they were nearly black, he moved her hands and ripped his own shirt off his chest.

The remainder of their clothing swiftly followed, until they faced each other with nothing covering their skin.

"Let me look at you," he said hoarsely. And she, with a soft, hesitant smile, let her arms drop to her sides and faced him.

The sight of her, so perfectly formed, nearly brought him to his knees.

Then, her soft smile widening, she took a step forward. "I'd like to do the same."

For a moment he didn't understand her whispered request. Then, when he realized she wanted to look at him as badly as he'd wanted to see her, he bit back a groan.

She came closer, circling him. When she pressed her naked breasts into his back, he shuddered. She kissed his neck and, with a savage cry, he turned so that his chest and hers, hard and soft, touched.

"Not yet," he told her. "I want to kiss you, here."

She began trembling as he tasted each taut nipple, and her moan of ecstasy nearly undid him. When she began stroking him, tentatively at first, then growing bolder, he burned under the feel of her hands on him.

He touched her, too, the sweet honey of her body more temptation than he could bear.

The couch seemed impossibly distant, but, half carrying her, he tumbled onto it. She sank into the buttery-soft leather as he buried himself in her.

Finally.

They fitted together perfectly.

Utterly and completely right.

Maybe now, he told himself with the last shred of co-herence remaining to him, once he'd slaked his hunger, he'd stop burning.

She kissed him again, her open mouth and the movement of her body a heady invitation as they moved together. He started to close his eyes, but then opened them. He wanted to watch her beautiful face, see the expression in her eyes as they danced together to the music she'd played for them both.

He burned, she shattered. As she did, he felt his own release begin and realized an awful truth. Rather than easing the way he burned for her, the fire had spread. She'd managed to enflame not only his body, but his heart and soul, as well.

He was, Chase thought, as he cradled her in his arms, in big trouble. The kind of trouble he not only didn't need, but after the fiasco with Kayla, had vowed never to let happen to him again.

* * *

The next morning, Chase went down to get coffee, leaving Sydney still asleep in his bed. He smiled when he remembered how they'd hastily dressed after the first time they'd made love, and then headed from the library to his room. He'd felt giddy, like a young kid. Giggling, she'd been the same. They'd whispered and exchanged breathless kisses while they'd slunk down the long hall.

Once they'd reached his room, she'd laughed so hard she'd fallen back onto his bed. He'd dived on top of her and they'd ended up in each other's arms again.

The laughter had changed to kisses, the kisses had led to caresses, and before long he was buried deep inside her, while she moved seductively under him.

She hadn't intended to stay the night; he hadn't intended to let her. They'd cuddled and he'd thought their lovemaking over, but a short while later, her tentative touches had him fully aroused again.

Amazing. Astounding. And absolutely, perfectly, fulfilling.

After a third marathon session in each other's arms, they'd both fallen deeply asleep. When he'd wakened to an armful of still-slumbering Sydney, he'd felt more content than he'd ever felt in his life.

Content? Fulfilled? Such feelings horrified him, especially since he knew how quickly they could disappear and how badly he'd hurt afterwards.

So when he'd woken to find her cuddled in his arms, and realized he wanted to stay that way indefinitely, he'd slid from his bed without waking her, stumbled to the bathroom where he'd brushed his teeth and dragged a brush through his hair. Then he'd hurriedly dressed and left her sleeping in his bed.

The kitchen was crowded; the other men appeared to have just finished their breakfast. Bright sunlight streamed in through the window over the sink. Outside, he could see the lake, bluer than the cloudless sky, with only a few boats marring its perfect surface.

Sydney would like—no. Heading for the coffeepot, Chase ordered himself to stop thinking of Sydney. But the mere thought of her brought to mind how badly he wanted to return to his room and join her, naked under the covers.

"What's up with you?" William regarded him curiously, peering out from behind the morning paper. "You look unusually content this morning."

The other two men eyed Chase, as well.

Carlos broke into a grin. "No, he looks like a well-fed lion who's just brought down a gazelle. I'm betting this has something to do with the beauticious Ms. Conner."

Ignoring the dark-haired man, Chase looked at William, who shrugged and went back to his newspaper. Sitting next to him, Jim wisely kept his mouth shut, though his bemused expression told Chase exactly what he was thinking.

His contentment showed in his face. Damn it. Sydney had somehow softened him. He wasn't sure he could afford to be so weak.

Sydney. Again he could see her, long, silky legs tangled in the sheets. In his mind's eye, she stretched, her full breasts outthrust, begging for the touch of his hand, or mouth.

Hell, he had it bad.

"There he goes again," Carlos commented. "He has the look of a man in lo—"

"Don't even say it," Chase snapped. Despite his irritation, or maybe because of it, he caught himself longing for Chawder Island. At least it had been deserted.

He eyed the three men and shook his head. "You know, it seems like it should be about time for you guys to head back to the palace, don't you think?"

Again glancing up from his newspaper, William shrugged. "Look, Savage, we'd all like to get back to the excitement of the palace. But we can't. When Lord Carrington orders it, we'll go. Until then, we have orders to stay."

"Yeah," Carlos put in, his mouth full of muffin. "Even with things so messed up back in Silverton, they want us to stay here in the sticks. Can you imagine?"

Jim nodded glumly. "With all that's going on, you'd think our entire department would be on call."

"What's going on?" Chase asked.

With a grimace, Carlos pointed at the paper William was reading. "The newspapers are going crazy. Rumors about the prince's death are flying, varying from a drug overdose to suicide. The king is supposedly dying, Sydney is rumored to have wed Reginald, and some reports are speculating she'll take over instead of the duke."

"Which papers?"

Carlos named two or three, ending with their nemesis, *The Quiz*.

"Anything about my engagement?" He crossed his arms.

William answered. "Not yet. Maybe that'll make tomorrow's papers. And the next issue of *The Quiz* isn't out until Thursday."

Carlos drummed his fingers on the table. "I don't understand how the PR department let things get so out of hand in our absence."

Cursing, Chase raked his hand through his hair. He couldn't help but hear the unspoken implication in the other man's voice. He was head of public relations.

Because he wasn't there to head up damage control, the other men thought he was letting the department down. Hell, he couldn't blame them.

"I don't understand why Carrington didn't call me in." Eyeing a particularly lurid headline that stated Reginald was really alive and hiding out in China, he shook his head.

"You mean you don't have a choice?" William sounded skeptical. "I thought you were here because you wanted to be."

"I'm here because I was sent here. Like you. Don't you think I'd rather be back in the thick of things?" Even as he spoke, he wondered. Would he? If going back meant leaving Sydney behind, how would he feel?

Jim spoke up finally, leaning his elbows on the table. "What are you hearing from the inside?"

"Not much." William's grim look matched Chase's gut feeling. "Our coworkers are being unusually tight-lipped." Which meant Chase had trained them well. "But then, I'm not in the loop. The upper brass only tells us what they think we need to know, which is precious little."

The upper brass. That could only mean Carrington.

As if on cue, William's cell phone chirped. Answering, he spoke a few words before handing it to Chase. "His Grace wishes to speak with you."

Ah, talk about serendipity. Now he would get answers.

Carrington's first words were to ask if Chase was alone.

"I can be." He motioned for William and the others to leave the room. The other men obeyed immediately, muttering about the secretive upper brass and not bothering to hide their interest in the phone call.

When the door closed behind them, Chase stepped out onto the patio for extra privacy. He stood looking over the lake, cell phone in hand, and had a premonition his life was about to change. "Now I am. Go ahead."

"Chase, the news is not good." Since the duke was always straightforward in his communications, Chase wondered at the amount of stress his boss was under.

"I understand," he said.

The duke sighed. "In the short time you've been gone, things have gone from bad to worse. Momentously worse."

Since Carrington was the original optimist, known for his dry humor, this was unlike him.

His mind raced. Such pessimistic urgency meant something big was about to erupt, something the royal PR department needed to handle. Chase was a master at putting a good spin on just about anything. He gripped the cell phone, feeling his adrenaline surge. This was why he worked in PR. At times like this, he loved his job. He was needed and he was ready. "What is it?"

"Reginald was murdered." Carrington took a deep breath. "The autopsy revealed high levels of cocaine in his blood. As you know, he was a regular party animal. I told you that at first we thought he'd died of a drug overdose. But the digitalis indicated otherwise."

"Digitalis?"

"The cocaine was laced with it. It's a drug that strengthens the contraction of the heart muscle, slows the heart and helps eliminate fluid from body tissues. It's used to treat congestive heart failure."

"Did Reginald have a heart condition?"

"Not at all. The doctor said there have been several documented cases of it being used as a poison, but that's rare. The use of it is known mostly to physicians."

"Someone wanted it to look like an overdose." Chase's thoughts raced. Reginald's excesses had been well-known and well-documented, even if the king had turned a blind eye to them. "The killer must have hoped the cocaine would blind us to anything else."

"Exactly. And the toxicology reports show this was not pharmacy-grade digitalis. It can be extracted from a plant called foxglove. Not easy, according to the doctor, but it can be done. Someone deliberately poisoned him."

"So the consensus is that he was murdered?" Chase shouldn't have been so surprised. Reginald had made many enemies over the years. Add drugs and you were asking for trouble. "Any suspects?"

"Several. We've got people working on narrowing it down."

By *people,* Chase knew Carrington meant the Lazlo Group. Headed by Corbett Lazlo, a brilliant, enigmatic man few had actually seen, the Lazlo Group was an international team of highly skilled agents who specialized in handling delicate government situations. Their cases included locating and rescuing kidnapped royals, investigating "deaths" of political figures, and reacquiring stolen information and artifacts. The duke had recently hired them, with King Weston's permission.

"There's more." The weighty silence following this statement caused anxiety to knot in Chase's stomach. He cleared his throat and waited, wondering what could possibly be worse than murder.

Chapter 10

When Carrington spoke again, he sounded weary. "King Weston collapsed when they broke this news to us. He's been unconscious for over twenty-four hours now."

Chase swallowed. "Is it serious?"

"He's in a coma. Dr. Zara Smith, the topflight neurologist, has been called in. We're hoping it's not a brain tumor."

"Press conference?"

"Not on this. None of this can be leaked to the general public."

"Of course not." Chase understood what the duke wasn't saying. With the king out of commission and no heir to the throne, they needed to do all they could to keep chaos from erupting in Silvershire.

Damage control. His specialty. He needed to go back to Silverton and handle the PR. There would be press conferences, releases. There were a thousand things that would need immediate handling. They needed him. He was good. No, he thought without a trace of humility. He was the best.

"I can handle this. Send a plane for me. I'll be back as soon as—"

"No."

"No?" Chase couldn't believe what he was hearing. "I'm sorry? You don't want me back to handle the fallout?"

"No. We've got it handled."

Stunned, Chase couldn't find his voice for a moment. Finally, he cleared his throat. "All of it?"

"You stay there. You're needed to deal with that particular delicate situation. The last thing we need is war to erupt between Silvershire and Naessa."

"War?" Dumbfounded, Chase forced himself to relax his grip on the cell phone. If he squeezed it much harder, the damn thing would probably break. "Sir, with all due respect, Sydney is illegitimate. Her father's never publicly claimed her."

"Ah, but that's not to say he won't suddenly declare her his beloved daughter. It's happened. You'd be surprised at the things people in positions of power can view as expedient."

Chase tried again. "But I've seen the papers. You need me."

"Chase," Carrington chided. "You can stay in close conact with your staff. They can handle this, as long as you check in with them once in a while. Tell them to call you if anything major erupts that they can't handle."

After the latest fiasco because of his absence, Chase didn't want to take a chance. In times of disaster, times like this, a pro was needed. *He* was needed.

But his employer didn't seem to think so.

"I don't understand." He felt as though he were being

fired. "Send someone else to handle Sydney Conner. I really think—"

"No. You don't understand. I need you there, with her. In addition to what we've already discussed, we've found more e-mails on Reginald's computer. Mixed in with Sydney Conner's attempts to contact the prince about their baby, we've found other, more threatening e-mails. We're not sure who sent them, and they weren't from the same e-mail address Sydney used earlier, but they were attempting to blackmail the prince. Lucia Cordez is sorting them out now."

Threatening? Blackmail? Chase blinked. Sydney? No way. "Determining the e-mail address should be relatively simple."

"They're working on it."

"Surely you don't think Sydney…"

Again, Carrington sighed. "We don't know, but it's a distinct possibility. But only that, until we have more to go on. This entire situation with her has the potential for disaster."

Chase closed his eyes and bit back another curse. How would his boss feel when he learned what Chase had done? He knew he had no choice but to tell him; the story would hit the papers soon, if it hadn't already.

"Chase?" Carrington's voice brought him back to the telephone. "Are you there?"

"I am." He took a deep breath. "There's something I'd better tell you before it hits the papers." As quickly and succinctly as possible, Chase outlined his and Sydney's pretend engagement as of the day before.

"You did what?" The duke's voice reflected his shock. "I read that in one of the tabloids, but thought it was the

usual lies. My God, Chase. I know you take your job seriously, but this is going a bit too far."

"It'll help take the heat off her for now. Once all this
blows over, I'll announce we broke it off."

"What made you do it?"

"I don't know." But he did know. He'd seen the stark pain
in her eyes at the reporter's words. Not good. Sympathy and
public relations weren't a good combination.

"Well then," Carrington sounded positively gleeful, "you
should have no problem getting her to stay at Lake Lodan."

Restless, Chase began to pace. He hated feeling out of
the loop, cut off from the heart of the action. Away from
the palace. "She wants to go home."

"To Naessa? Not possible."

"True, but I'm running out of reasons to make her stay.
She's not a prisoner, and she hasn't been charged with any
crime. I can't hold her against her will."

"Charm her. As long as I've known you, women have
been climbing all over you."

The vivid imagery conjured by the duke's words made
Chase break out in a light sweat. Just thinking of last night
and the woman who still slept in his bed, made him feel in
need of an ice-cold shower. The burning, desperate passion
that had flared between him and Sydney had seared him.
He'd never felt anything like it.

Carrington spoke again. "Chase? Are you there? Is
there a problem with you charming the girl? I'd think you
two would be rather close now, especially after your
ordeal together."

Charming the girl? Earlier, when he'd believed
Sydney a groupie, Chase would have had no problem
doing just that. Now...he didn't know. Especially since

she'd totally freaked when he'd announced their pretend engagement.

"I don't think she likes me very much." His excuse sounded lame, even to his own ears. But it was the truth, though their bodies had reacted to each other like moths to a flame.

Carrington chuckled. "Right. You're engaged. After all, you forget how well I know you. Since when has a woman, any woman, not liked you? Come on, man. Where's that legendary charisma? You've been a player since I've known you, and that's a long time."

"She's…different." That was as close as he could come to explaining her effect on him.

"Different?" The duke's chuckles became an outright guffaw. "I've seen pictures of her. The woman's hot. You can deal with it. I have faith in you."

The words made Chase smile grimly. So far his orders were clear. Stay with Sydney, keep a watchful eye on her while keeping her safe and away from the press. A tall order, especially since he now had to worry about keeping her safe from himself.

Speaking of keeping her safe, he still had one very important question for the duke. "Speaking of Sydney, have the Lazlos learned who's trying to kill her?"

The duke was silent for so long, Chase wasn't sure he'd understood. When he finally spoke, he sounded pensive. "They're exploring various avenues."

"Not good enough," Chase snapped, before he caught himself. "Sorry."

Carrington accepted his apology with a quiet, "That's all right."

"Is there anything else you can tell me?"

"No, not really. I can't elaborate yet. Just as with Reginald, there are several factions who might have good reason to want her—and the baby she carries—dead. That's why your engagement, even if it's pretend, is a risky move." A trace of humor colored Carrington's voice, as though he had his own suspicions about why Chase had done such a thing.

"Oh? How so?"

"If there is someone out there gunning for Sydney Conner, you've just linked yourself with her. You could be a target now."

"Why Carrington," Chase used his most droll tone. "I didn't know you cared."

The duke ignored the feeble attempt at humor. "Of course I care, you big idiot. You're a great PR guy—and an even better friend."

Chase had to swallow to get past the lump in his throat. "Don't forget, I was a bodyguard. I know how to handle threats. Still, I'd be interested to see what the Lazlo Group turns up."

"I'll call you as soon as I learn anything. But for now, I want you to keep an eye on her, charm her, befriend her, do whatever you have to to keep her there, out of the spotlight, away from the media. Once all is said and done, if she's innocent of nothing worse than sleeping with Reginald, we'll give her the same settlement we originally intended."

The settlement he now carried in his wallet. A certified bank check made out in the amount of seven hundred and fifty thousand pounds.

Pay her to go away. That's what Chase had been sent to do in the beginning, when someone had started shooting at them. The amount of money he'd been given to bribe her was staggering to him, but would Sydney, with her trust fund, find it so?

"Chase?"

Blinking, he cleared his throat. "Got it."

"Fantastic. Until then, watch your back." With that final warning, Carrington rang off.

Chase knew he'd have to watch more than his back. He had to make sure his heart wasn't involved.

Sydney woke alone in Chase's bed. Outside the open window, she heard the sound of a child's laughter. Smiling, certain she'd imagined the cheery noise, she yawned, wondering why her body felt so sore.

Then the truth hit her.

She'd slept with Chase. Actually, they'd done very little sleeping. She'd finally given in to her craving and made love with him.

What had she done? Hand to her throat, she trembled. Their coming together had been unlike anything she'd ever experienced before. Worse, merely thinking of his kiss, his touch, and she longed for him again.

Stretching, she winced. Despite feeling as though she glowed from within, she ached in places she'd never ached before. Her entire body blushed when she thought of the sensual way they'd devoured each other.

Chase Savage, sent by the royal family to deal with a "problem." Her. Now, being with him was a bittersweet reminder that she didn't learn from her mistakes. First Reginald, and now Chase.

Ah, but Chase… Before, she'd only wondered how she'd live without him once she went home. Now, she knew. Nothing would ever be the same. And the worst part of it all—she wished her baby's father had been Chase instead of Reginald.

Sitting up and combing her hair with her fingers, she wondered if mistakes, like bad luck, came in threes. If so, she could only wonder what her third blunder would be.

Sighing, she tossed back the covers and located her clothes. Once dressed, she made her way back to her room and her shower.

Later, clean and wearing her favorite pair of faded jeans, Sydney made her way to the kitchen. At the sound of Chase's deep voice, she froze and, her face heating, changed direction. Though her stomach felt hollow, she'd get something to break her fast later, when the kitchen was deserted.

Outside, the sunlight looked warm and welcoming. She slipped out into the side garden and found a worn, wooden bench next to the rose arbor, partly in the morning sun. With a pleased sigh, she sat down, leaned back and closed her eyes.

"When the sun hits it just right, your hair looks like it's on fire."

Sydney opened her eyes to see a slender, dark-haired child studying her with solemn eyes. Five or six years old, she clutched a battered stuffed animal to her thin chest.

"Hello. What's your name?" She squatted so she was at the child's level.

"Martha." Trusting, the little girl stepped forward and held out her hand. "May I touch your hair?"

Sydney laughed. "Of course you can." Once Martha had finished patting her head, Sydney stood. "What are you doing here?"

With a bright smile, Martha pointed toward the door. "My babysitter's sick, so I came to work with my mama."

Giggling, she ran to the rosebush and sniffed a flower. "I'd rather stay outside and play than stay with her."

Sydney got up and took the child's hand. "Does your mother know you're out here?"

The little girl only shrugged. Then, frowning, she pointed to the sky. "Look, it's going to rain!"

Dark storm clouds were indeed rolling in. Even as Sydney watched, they overtook the sun, plunging Martha and her into shadows.

Despite her terror of storms, Sydney refused to be distracted. "Where is your mother, Martha?"

Martha sighed. Her little nose wrinkled. "In the kitchen, helping the cook. That's where she works. But it's really hot in there. I like it way better out here. Especially now," she sniffed the air like a curious puppy. "It smells like rain. I love to play in the rain."

And all Sydney could think about was how badly she wanted to hide. "I know you like it out here." The wind had picked up, whipping Sydney's hair around her face.

Martha lifted her arms to the sky and twirled. "Don't you?"

"Not really." Sydney tugged her forward, toward the house. "Tell you what. Let's go find your mom. If she says it's okay for you to be with me, I'll see if I can find a book to read you. They have a huge library here."

"Really?"

Because the child sounded so amazed, Sydney chuckled. "Really."

"But I want to play outside."

Shivering in earnest, Sydney shook her head. "Not if there's a bad storm. Coming outside wouldn't be safe then."

"Are you scared?"

Sydney couldn't lie to the child. "Yes, I am." Cocking her head, Martha studied her, small mouth pursed with fascination. "A little."

In the distance, thunder sounded. Sydney shuddered. "A lot. I don't like storms." She held out her hand. Martha took it, still studying Sydney's face.

"Why?"

"I nearly drowned once. A storm came up when I was on a sailboat. The boat turned over." She wouldn't tell the child she'd been trapped underneath the sail, nor that her mother had made no effort to save her. If not for a shift in the wind and the man who'd been her mother's paramour of the moment, Sydney had no doubt she would have drowned.

As if she understood, Martha nodded. Clutching Sydney's hand, she went along docilely, as though she didn't mind going inside.

Instead, as soon as Sydney reached for the door, Martha pulled her hand loose and took off running, giggling as she ran. "My mommy says the best way to deal with a fear is to face it." As she ran, lightning flashed above them and the sky darkened to the color of pre-dawn.

Stunned, at first Sydney simply stood frozen, one hand on the door. Then, as the little girl dashed out of sight, she took off after her, pushing away her instinctive terror to the back of her mind.

Martha wanted to play and clearly did not understand the danger. Because she was the only adult around, Sydney thought, as she chased the little girl out into the wide-open expanse of lawn on the north side of the property, she had a responsibility to bring the child to safety.

When she caught up with Martha, she'd reached the end of the yard. Holding on to the tall, iron fence with one hand,

Martha grinned up at her as Sydney came running up. Heart pounding, all Sydney could think of was how metal attracted lightning.

Still, she knew she couldn't reveal the extent of her terror to the little girl.

"Hey, you," Sydney gasped, out of breath. "I caught you." She reached to pry Martha's hand away from the fence. If she had to, she'd drag her kicking and screaming inside.

The first spatters of rain hit her face.

"Oh goody! It's going to pour!" Martha took off again. Grabbing for her arm, Sydney narrowly missed.

Thunder boomed. Instinctively, Sydney cringed, cursing. The precious second allowed Martha to gain ground. For a second she appeared to be considering a headlong dash in the opposite direction, back toward the house. Then, staring down at the lake below, she seemed to change her mind, skidding to a stop.

Not wanting to spook her, Sydney slowed to a walk, moving closer, hoping to grab Martha while the girl's attention was elsewhere.

"Look!" Martha pointed.

Closer, Sydney pretended to have seen. "I see that." She was nearly there.

"No, you don't." Martha danced away. "You've got to look."

"Fine." Shading her eyes with her hand, Sydney tried to see what had caught the child's attention. "I'm looking. Look at what?"

"That bird." Pointing, the little girl scrunched up her face. "I want to touch it."

Following the direction of Martha's finger, Sydney saw

a small white swan swimming near the shore below them. "It's pretty, isn't it?"

"I want to touch it," Martha repeated.

Closer. Ten feet. Eight. "Well, you can't. First off, there's no way down there. Secondly, it would probably swim away if you got near—"

Before Sydney could finish the sentence, Martha took off, disappearing over the edge of the cliff.

For a second Sydney's heart stopped. She stared, disbelieving. Then, as her heart resumed pumping, she rushed to the edge and saw a narrow, worn path twisting down the cliff to the lakeshore. Moving with the utter carefree carelessness of the very young, Martha was about a third of the way down.

Thunder boomed. A millisecond later, another bolt of lightning flashed, lighting up the sky. The rain came in sheets, driven by the wind.

Below, Martha screamed in terror. She lost her footing and began to slide, shrieking as she tried to grab hold of something to stop her rapid decent. But she couldn't and Sydney caught a glimpse of her terrified little face as she plunged down, then hit the lake with a splash. She bobbed up, then disappeared under the water as a jagged bolt of lightning flashed above them.

With no choice, Sydney went after her.

Chapter 11

There were days when Lake Lodan looked like a postcard from paradise, all sparkling, calm water and clear, robin's-egg skies. Days when the sun enticed, the breeze beckoned, and the sailboats presented a picture of serenity and ease.

Today, Chase reflected, was not one of those days. He walked as close to the cliff's edge as he dared and stared out at the now-deserted lake. Above, the sky darkened as storm clouds gathered, roiling black and gray, and the wind carried the threat of more than mere rain. A wicked storm was brewing, and there'd be nothing subtle about this one.

Standing on the edge of the cliff, Chase thrilled to the electric feeling in the air. Unlike Sydney, he'd always loved storms. Even when he'd been a child, his mother'd had to drag him inside, away from both thunderstorms and bliz-zards. The savagery of nature's fury fascinated him. Today, with his insides in as much turmoil as the weather, the coming storm would be a welcome distraction.

The sound of the choppy waves slamming against the rocks mirrored the sky. With the barometric pressure dropping and his nerve endings tingling from the electricity in the air, all he could see was Sydney's face.

Remembering her terror of storms, he wondered if he should go to her. Without a shadow of a doubt, he knew she'd be inside, trying to hide her fear. He could imagine wrapping her in his arms for comfort and stealing one kiss. Vivid images of what that kiss would lead to had him shifting restlessly.

Better to avoid her, let her deal with the weather in her own way. He needed to clear his head.

Though he'd known her less than a month, he couldn't stop thinking about her. Aching for her, wanting her, craving her. Prince Reginald's discarded mistress.

Sydney.

Leaning heavily on the wooden railing, he peered glumly at the restless lake and released a shuddering breath. What was it about this woman that affected him so? How was she different from the dozens of others, equally beautiful, equally sexy, he'd known?

He had no answer. He only knew she was. Everything about her, from the top of her fiery head to the delicate shape of her perfect toes, enticed him. After their one night of passion, he'd thought his hunger for her would be slaked, and therefore lessened. Instead, this one night had given him all the more reason to burn for her.

They fitted together like a hand in a glove. A very soft, very snug, leather glove, he thought. When they'd been together, he'd felt more than lust. When they'd reached the peak of release, he'd felt more than sexual fulfillment. Much more. Too much more.

Damn it. He tightened his hand around the smooth iron rail. This one woman, Sydney Conner, had him dreaming again of the possibility of enjoying a life like his parents. He thought of his mother and father, of their obvious affection for each other, the love they shared, passed out indiscriminately to each of their boisterous brood.

Each of his siblings had found love, married and they were raising their own children. Of all the Savage brood, Chase was the only one who'd chosen to devote his life to a career rather than domestic contentment.

Because of Kayla. When she'd shown him his foolish dreams weren't possible, he'd thrown himself into his work with all the passion he would have brought to their marriage.

And never, not once, had he ever questioned his choice. Until now. Now he could swear he saw nothing but a gnawing emptiness stretching out before him.

Until he'd met Sydney and contemplated an existence without her, he'd never felt alone.

Now, the prospect of returning home each night to his professionally decorated and very empty apartment in downtown Silverton seemed too high a price to pay, even for a job he loved.

Chase was, he knew, indulging in foolishness. Foolish dreams were for other men, not him. No doubt he'd feel more like himself once he got back in his familiar environment.

Not wanting to examine his new emotions any closer, he shook his head and lifted his face to the moist wind. Here came the storm. He waited for the familiar excitement to fill him, but worry for Sydney superceded it.

Once, he'd been a bodyguard. Protecting others was ingrained in him. Even now as head of PR, finally on the right track career-wise, he seemed poised to take a wrong turn, an unnecessary detour back in time.

And he couldn't seem to stop, to resist Sydney's potent lure. He felt like a man drowning.

Startled out of his musing by a strange sound, he cocked his head and listened again. Below, the noise came again, a child's shrill shriek. He peered down at the shore, trying to locate the source of the cry.

There, below, near the choppy water's edge. In disbelief, he watched a small black-headed girl slide down the cliff, arms flailing as she tried to regain her balance. A second later, her high-pitched scream was cut off as she slipped and the water swallowed her.

He started forward, running. When he'd inspected the grounds at their arrival, he'd spotted an old path on the other side of the house. He ran for that now, keeping an eye on the water below, desperately praying the child would reappear.

Thunder crackled. Lightning flashed. The sky opened up.

Below, Sydney appeared: running, stumbling down the rocky beach. Reaching the spot where the girl had gone under, she climbed up onto a rock. Then, without hesitation, she jumped into the wind-tossed waves after the little girl.

Chase's heart stopped. There—the path. As he scrabbled down the rocky cliff side, he could only pray he wasn't too late to save them both.

Sydney emerged from the water just as he reached the cliff bottom. He moved as fast as he could to her, careful on the slippery rocks. When she spotted him, she tried to hand him the water-soaked little girl and failed.

Around them, the storm reached a crescendo of fury.

He jumped in, took the child from Sydney's arms, and made his way over the rocks to a grassy area on the shore. Laying the little girl down, he turned to go back for Sydney and saw she'd climbed out after him.

The rain lashed at him as Chase turned his attention to the small girl. He began CPR until she coughed, a heaving, hacking sound, and all the water she'd taken in came up.

Lightning illuminated her tiny, limp body.

"She's breathing," Sydney said, her teeth chattering. "Martha's breathing."

"Sydney?" He spared her a glance. She'd wrapped her arms around herself as though she could conjure a towel. Huge shudders shook her and she looked on the verge of shock.

"Y-y-yes?"

"Run for the house and call for an ambulance. We need to get Martha to a hospital as soon as possible."

Before he'd finished, Sydney took off. A moment later, Chase lifted the unconscious child and began the arduous climb to the house.

Later, as the storm moved away and the paramedics wheeled the now-alert child out, followed by her grateful mother, Chase looked for Sydney. He found her, damp clothes clinging to her, staring out the window at the lingering rain.

Without a sound, he slipped up behind her and wrapped her tightly in his arms. Motionless, she accepted his wordless comfort, laying her head against his chest. Together they stood and watched the remainder of the storm batter the lake.

He felt a sense of completion, of fulfillment, more different and exhilarating than he'd ever felt with a woman before. Once again, he ignored the doubt raising its ugly head, and chose to live in the moment.

She shivered. He kissed her neck.

"That was really brave."

"Not really. Anyone would have done the same." Though her tone was unremarkable, when she looked at him, he saw remembered terror stark in her eyes.

"Brave," he insisted, nuzzling under her ear. She turned into him, hiding her face. "For you even to be out there, with your thing about storms, is remarkable. And that little girl owes you her life."

"No. Not me. You saved her. You brought her up out of the water and did CPR." Shuddering again, she shook her head and held on to him as though her life depended on it. In turn, he wrapped his arms around her and found himself wishing he never had to let her go.

That night, Chase visited Sydney's room. Awake as though waiting for him, she welcomed him with a sleepy smile and open arms.

After another blissful night filled with sensual pleasures, chest tight, he lay and watched her sleeping. Finally, he rose and returned to his own room, leaving her alone in her bed.

The next morning, a newspaper had been slid under his door. Several more had been stacked neatly in the hall. Curious, Chase retrieved them, opening each one to see, with little surprise, that his and Sydney's engagement had made the front pages of them all. Most were guardedly optimistic, though several took a unique spin on what should have been a happy event.

Illegitimate Princess's Newest Scandal, *The Quiz*'s

headline screamed. A few other tabloids picked up similar themes, many accusing Sydney of lying about her baby belonging to the prince when she had obviously gotten pregnant with Chase.

He sighed. From the moment he'd opened his mouth, he'd expected no less. Now he had to deal with the consequences of his impulsive actions.

A cold shower helped him think more clearly. He'd barely finished drying off when his mother called. She'd seen the headlines.

"Why didn't you tell us?" She sounded hurt. In the background he could hear his sisters chattering, laughing, and scolding their kids.

"Mom, I was going to call." As soon as he figured out what to say. He supposed he ought to tell his family the truth, but he couldn't risk someone slipping up. As far as the press and the rest of the world needed to know, he and Sydney really were engaged.

"When did this happen? How long have you been seeing this girl?" She fired questions, one after the other, without even giving him time to answer. To her credit, she didn't mention Kayla, or how he'd been left standing at the altar the very day of his planned wedding.

When his mother paused to take a breath, he interjected. "It was a sudden thing. Impulsive."

"Impulsive? Marriage should never be done on impulse. It's a lifelong commitment." Her rebuke was soft, but no less heartfelt. She and his father had been married forty years this past autumn.

Knowing she was right, he pushed away a stab of guilt. It was only an engagement, after all. It wasn't as if he'd actually married Sydney under false pretenses.

"When are we going to meet her?"

"When?" He glanced at his watch. "I don't know. Things are hectic at work right now. But soon, okay?"

His mother sighed. "Hold on. Your sister wants to talk to you."

Chase tensed. Which sister? His eldest sister had taken on the role of official family spokesperson. This couldn't be good.

When his older sister, Sarah, came on, he knew he was in for it.

"I'm concerned." She began without preamble. Her tone was sharp. "We're all worried about you. This woman was sleeping with the prince right up until he died."

What could he say? "I know, but it's complicated."

"Complicated?" She snorted. "I've seen pictures of her. Are you thinking clearly, or not thinking at all?"

As he tried to collect his thoughts, there was a soft knock at his door.

Thanking the interruption, he murmured his apologies and, along with a promise to phone back later, disconnected the call, much to his sister's irritation. "Come in."

"Good morning." Sydney peeked her head around the door. Her bright smile faded when she saw all the papers. "What's going on?"

"Take a look." He handed her the *Inquisitor*. "Might as well start with the worst one first."

"And we had the misfortune of making this week's issue." She shook her head, a tiny frown appearing between her eyebrows as she began reading.

When she'd finished, she worried her lower lip. "I don't like this."

"I know." He suppressed the urge to hold her, knowing

if he touched her they'd end up right back in bed. "Don't worry. This won't last long. If we stay out of their radar, they'll lose interest and hound someone else."

"I know." With a grimace, she tossed the papers back onto his bed.

"Sydney?"

"Hmmm?" She looked up expectantly.

"Let's talk about you and Reginald."

Just like that, her expression shut down. "Why?"

"Because I knew him," he said. "He was a partier and a player. Between the booze and the drugs, not to mention his harem, I'm trying to understand how someone like you ended up with someone like him."

Moving as though each of his words had been cuts, she crossed the room and took a seat on the edge of his bed. "He said my love had changed him." She sounded disgusted. "I know—oldest line in the book, and I believed it. Looking back now, I think I was dazzled."

"Because of who he was?"

Before he'd even finished, she shook her head. "No, not because of that. Though you might find this hard to believe, I've never cared about such things. My sire still pays for my mother's house and her lavish lifestyle, but he never paid me a visit. Reginald dazzled me with attention. I thought—" she swallowed, looking away for a moment before her bright-blue gaze found his "—he really cared. Of course, he didn't."

Her bitter voice increased his longing to hold her. She'd said the last sentence in a way that told him she didn't believe she was worthy of Reginald's love.

Reginald hadn't been worthy to touch the hem of her skirt.

Oblivious to his rage, Sydney shook her head and continued. "Now, I realize I never truly knew him."

Chase bit back the retort on his tongue and watched her, trying to keep his distance, trying not to feel. If he closed his eyes, all he could see was the prince with his hands on her soft, silky skin. Furious, Chase fought the urge to touch her, to purge the image from his mind.

Instead, he crossed his arms and fought himself. The need to protect her warred with his desire to understand.

Then, though he really didn't want to know, he asked. "Tell me how you met."

Watching him with shuttered eyes, she sighed. "You must have read the papers. Sometimes I think Reginald staged the entire thing. He came backstage when the symphony played in Silverton for a month. He brought red roses and clever promises. I told him no. He came again the next night. And the next, and the one after that. Always with the roses and the honeyed words. Each time, he grew more and more extravagant. I found him amusing, at first. But he was a prince, like my sire. I should have known better."

"What changed?" Chase heard the harshness in his voice and made an effort to soften his tone. "You were a virgin, untouched. How could you let a man like that—" He swallowed, bit back his words. Then, when he thought he had himself under control again, he continued. "What did he do to make you agree to become his lover?"

She gave him a sharp look. "Nothing happened overnight. He kept it up for weeks, Chase. Weeks. When our stay in Silverton ended and the symphony moved on, he came, too. He traveled from city to city, wherever we played. And finally, one night when he asked me to dinner, I went. I remember thinking at the time how it was only a simple meal. How much harm could it possibly cause?" She bit her lip and gave a self-conscious laugh. "Little did I know."

Did she sound wistful, or sad? Suddenly, he realized he didn't want to hear any more. The intimate details of Sydney and Reginald's affair were none of his business, none of his concern. The fact that hearing about them made him want to punch the wall was another reason.

She had him tied up in knots. Like Kayla, he told himself. Best if he remembered how that had ended.

Ah, but Sydney was still talking.

"We started having dinner together two, maybe three times a week. Then he showed up on my day off and wanted to take me on a picnic."

"No shopping? I thought guys like that bought their lady friends lots of bling."

"He tried to give me jewelry. But I didn't want to ever be like my mother, so I refused to accept his gifts. But I'd come to enjoy his company. Reginald can—" She stopped herself, swallowed and continued. "Could, I mean. Reginald could be a very charming man when he wanted to. When we had our picnic, he brought a basket with cheese and crackers and pâté and wine. He spread a blanket on the ground for me to sit on. And then—"

He saw red, but couldn't keep himself from asking. "Then what? You had sex?"

"No, Chase. He kissed me. I enjoyed the kiss. We went on this way for a month."

Why the hell did this feel like a betrayal? As though she'd cheated on him? Disgusted, Chase tried to catch his breath, to calm himself. He hadn't even known her then. And worse, she didn't seem to realize what she was saying, how every word cut him and made him desire her more for her naive need.

The prince had been notorious for his rapid conquests.

The mere fact that she'd been able to resist him had no doubt fueled his interest.

"Men always seem to want the one thing they can't have."

He wasn't aware he'd spoken out loud until Sydney answered him. "And then once they've obtained it, they don't want it anymore." She clasped and unclasped her hands. "I thought he cared, Chase. Shows you how incredibly stupid I was. When he got tired of me, he moved right on to the next woman."

The words she didn't say echoed in his mind. Leaving her pregnant with his baby.

"What kind of man doesn't care about his own child?" Her anguish was palpable. "I couldn't believe it when he pretended not to know me. He deleted my e-mails, refused delivery of my certified letter. He didn't want to hear that I was pregnant. He wanted me to go away."

He couldn't take any more. With an oath, he crossed the room and pulled her into his arms. "I'm sorry, Sydney. I shouldn't have asked."

"I—"

"Shh." He kissed the top of her head, promising himself he'd keep things chaste. But she turned in his arms and, facing him, pushed herself to her knees. Dragging his face down to hers, she kissed him, desperately using her tongue and her lips to drive all thoughts of her with the other man out of his head.

The only other words she said before they sank in a tangle of covers and sheets and skin was to comment, "How very convenient we're on your bed."

Then he kissed her again and neither spoke for a very long time.

* * *

The sound of alarms going off woke them. Chase opened his eyes, shifting Sydney from on top of him. She sat up, her glorious hair tangled, blinking in confusion.

"What's wrong? Is there a fire?"

"I don't know." He tugged her to her feet, feeling his door for heat before opening it. "I need to get you outside." Yanking open the door, he pulled her, stumbling, into the smoke-filled hallway. "Come on."

"But what about William, Jim and Carlos? We need to find them."

Still dragging her, he cursed. "No, *I* need to find them, once I'm sure you're safe."

Just then, William came running up, motioning frantically. "This way. We need to get outside."

Single-file, they held on to each other as they made their way blindly down the hall. Chase kept Sydney in front of him, close.

"What about the others?" he asked.

"I sent Carlos and Jim to round up the servants. They should already be out."

"Good. I don't want to lose anyone."

"We shouldn't. The alarms warned us in time."

Sydney coughed, her eyes watering in the thick smoke. Chase yanked off his black Armani T-shirt. "Take this. Hold it over your face."

Her gaze searched his. "But what about you?"

"I'll be fine." He pushed her gently. "Now move."

They reached the back door a few seconds later. William shoved it open and they all stumbled outside, gasping in the fresh air. Sydney rubbed her eyes and her hands came away black with soot.

Keeping one arm around her, Chase faced the other man. "Have you seen the fire?"

"No," William admitted. "Just a lot of smoke. The fire department's on its way. I've called for the police, as well."

A few minutes later, the fire engine pulled up, lights flashing, sirens wailing. A police cruiser accompanied it, though the officers remained outside while the firefighters did their job.

Afterward the fire captain emerged with something in his hand, motioning to the policemen. Chase went, too. Sydney followed.

"No fire. Someone set off a couple of these." He held up a blackened, empty metal tube.

"What is it?" Chase asked.

"Smoke bombs." Both the fire captain and the police officer spoke at the same time. "Homemade, from the looks of them. Potassium nitrate and sugar, mainly. Cook it and stuff these tubes with it, add a safety fuse and, voila—you get a ton of thick smoke."

"Why?" Sydney had meant to stay quiet, but the instant she blurted the question, they all turned to look at her. "Why would they want to smoke us out?"

The policeman shook his head. "I don't know."

Chase blanched. "To get you outside. Damn, we've been played for fools." Ignoring the uncomprehending looks on the other's faces, he herded Sydney toward the gardening shed and greenhouse, shielding her with his body. While they moved fast, he constantly watched, searching the area for anything out of the ordinary. William, Jim and Carlos were right behind him.

Scratching his head, the uniformed officer followed.

Once they reached the greenhouse, Chase tried the door.

It was locked. With a hard shove of his shoulder, he rammed it. The thin wood gave way, splintering.

"Come on." Chase led Sydney inside. "Though they can see you through the glass, this offers some protection. William, Jim, Carlos—form a circle around Sydney. We'll protect her with our bodies. Anyone wanting to take a shot at her will have to go through us first."

"Sir?" The cop stood in the doorway, peering at them in the murky light. "Would you care to clarify that comment?"

Chase measured the shorter man with a quick, hard look. "Not just yet. But if I have need of your services, officer, I'll let you know."

As the officer was about to speak, someone from the group still assembled on the back lawn screamed.

Chapter 12

The cop spun and sprinted for the crowd. Sydney started forward, but Chase grabbed her and pulled her back into the shadowy humidity of the greenhouse. Leafy ferns sheltered them. "No," he growled. "Don't move."

William and the other two men hadn't budged. Sydney fought the urge to push at them and make them get out of the way.

"We need to go see what happened. That sounded like someone was hurt."

"Let the cops deal with it. We're staying here. If there's a sniper with his weapon trained on the crowd, who do you think he's looking for?"

She stared, the color draining from her already pale face. "Here? Inside the gate?"

Without answering her rhetorical question, he turned to

look at the other men. "William, Carlos, check out the house. Jim, stay with me. We need to keep Sydney between us."

William and Carlos disappeared inside. Jim stepped closer, keeping his back to Sydney while he scanned their surroundings. The cop never returned.

A few minutes later, they heard another siren.

"Ambulance," Chase told her. "That's a good sign. If whoever got shot was dead, they wouldn't bother to call an ambulance."

Sydney glanced at her watch. "What's keeping William and Carlos? Surely they could have checked out the house by now."

Jim and Chase exchanged a look. When Chase glanced down at Sydney, he was smiling. "They're very thorough. They won't be back until they're a hundred-percent positive the house is safe."

Nodding, Jim grinned at them both. "You trained them well, sir."

"If you have a moment, I'd like to talk to all of you." The police officer had returned, looking grim. "There's been a shooting. The woman is en route to the hospital."

"Was she badly hurt?" Sydney tried to step around Chase, but he moved enough to make that impossible.

The cop looked from one to the other, his expression hard. "She was shot in the back. They were able to get her stabilized. Other than that, I couldn't say."

"Did she have red hair?"

Instead of answering, the police officer jerked his thumb toward the house. "Let's go inside. I have a few questions for you. All of you."

William and Carlos stepped through the door. The small greenhouse was becoming quite crowded.

"All safe," William said.

"Let's take her in now." Chase didn't even have to ask them before the other two men stepped around the cop to flank Sydney.

Seeing this, the policeman moved to block the doorway. "What's going on here?"

Chase merely looked at him.

"Answer the question!"

"You didn't answer mine. In case you didn't hear me, I'll repeat it. Did the woman who was shot have red hair?"

"Yes," the cop growled. "She was one of the cooks or maids. Are you saying the shooter might have been aiming for her?" He jerked his thumb at Sydney.

Heaving a sigh, Chase glanced at the house before looking the officer full in the face. "Yes. We think someone is targeting my fiancée."

From the way he referred to her, Sydney deduced he knew all of this would make the news. She inhaled softly, but kept quiet while Chase finished.

"From the back, someone might have thought the staff member resembled the princess. Now, will you get out of our way so we can get her in the house?"

Finally, the cop stepped aside. He followed them as they moved in a tight knot of bodies and opened the door for them when they reached the house.

Once inside, Chase politely answered his questions. Watching, Sydney noticed how he used his public relations training to put his own spin on the truth.

Finally, she could take no more. "Sir?"

They all looked at her.

"We'd like to keep this out of the media, if possible."

Though Chase and his men shook their heads, smiling,

the policeman took her seriously. "I can promise you those reporters won't learn anything from me, ma'am." He closed his notepad and stepped back. "Looks like I'm done here. The crime-scene guys will be a while wrapping things up outside."

Chase nodded. "My man will show you to the door."

"What about protection?" the cop asked. "I'll request beefed-up patrols of the area."

"Good. Palace security will be called in, as well." This seemed to satisfy the officer. Still grim-faced, he left.

"Now." Chase looked at his men. "We need a security detail on the premises. Call the duke and arrange it."

Without another word, William hurried away.

Exhausted, Sydney couldn't think. Couldn't move, couldn't speak. Chase was right. Someone really *was* trying to kill her. She sank down on the sofa and leaned her head back, wishing she dared to close her eyes.

A moment later, William returned. "I left the duke a message to call me back."

"At least I kept all this from the media," Sydney told them.

All the men laughed.

"I doubt that." Still chuckling, Chase dropped on to the couch beside her.

"But he promised…"

"Just wait. First time someone waves a television camera in his face, he'll spill his guts. I've seen it happen a hundred times."

"But—"

The doorbell rang. They all froze.

Sydney clung to Chase. Firmly, he pried her fingers off his arm. "Stay here."

Pushing himself off the couch, he went to the front

door and stood to the side while he looked through the peephole. "I don't see anything." He reached for the door handle to open it.

"Don't." Sydney jumped up and started forward. "Chase, please."

"Get back. If there's someone watching out there, he'll be gunning for you." Something glinted in his hand. A gun. A weapon she hadn't even known he had.

Slowly he opened the front door.

Martha, the little daughter of the cook's helper, stood shivering on the doorstep. As soon as she saw Chase, she burst into tears.

Quickly, he drew her inside. She ran to Sydney, still sobbing. "That was my mama the bad man shot. They took her to the hospital and wouldn't let me go with her."

Sydney held her, smoothing back her hair. "I'm sure she'll be all right." She wasn't sure of anything at this point.

"I want to see my mother," Martha wailed. "Why'd they take her away?"

"To make her well, honey."

With sniffles and hiccups, Martha began to take notice of the others in the room. She straightened. "There's lots of people here."

Sydney smiled at Chase over the child's dark head. "Yes, there are."

"Policemen and firemen and ambulance drivers." Wiping at her eyes, Martha sniffed. "And the bad man."

Chase froze. "The bad man?"

Vigorously, the little girl nodded. She lifted one chubby hand to reveal a crumpled paper clenched in her fist. "He gave me this to give to you, Princess Sydney."

Heart racing, Sydney took it, smoothing the paper

against the arm of her chair. Keeping one arm around the little girl, she digested the words silently, before handing it to Chase.

He read it out loud. "'Watch your back and look for the way out. Or your bastard won't live long enough to claim the throne.'"

William frowned. "That doesn't sound like a threat. More like a warning." Chase agreed.

"But from whom? And why? I have no aspiration to the throne." Sydney glanced around the room, noting all the windows. Then Martha began weeping again, and Sydney busied herself calming her. Finally, the cook, who turned out to be Martha's aunt, came to take the little girl and put her down for a much-needed nap. Chase made a mental note to ask her later, when she'd calmed, what the bad man looked like and how she knew he was bad.

The rest of that afternoon, every random sound startled Sydney. The simple cry of a crow, the gentle clunk of the air conditioner when it kicked on, the lake breeze sending a tree branch scraping against the window, all became a reason to suspect someone was out there lurking. Stalking her.

Her fear was mostly for her unborn baby. More than anything else, she wished Reginald had not been the father. If he hadn't, no one would be after her.

"Would you like to come with me?" Chase, sensing her unease, squeezed her shoulder. "We're going to review the security videos."

"Yes." She hadn't even realized there were security cameras. Of course there were. This was the royal lake house after all.

But this time the expensive surveillance equipment hadn't done its work.

"The front-door camera went dead for fifty-eight seconds." Chase shook his head. "Not good."

"Blank tape. Nothing," the head of security said. A large, rawboned man of sixty-odd years, he had the look of a former police officer. "Same as the ones that were focused on the front gates."

"The fire, the shooting, then what?" wondered Chase. "When he realized he'd shot the wrong woman, he came back to give the little girl a note?"

"Maybe he stuck around," William suggested. "This place has a ton of servants."

"Or," Carlos put in, "maybe there's two of them."

"Two of them." Chase appeared to be mulling over this theory. "One bad guy, one good?"

"Maybe one bad guy, one not so bad." Carlos indicated the note in Chase's hand. "I still think whoever gave that note to little Martha is trying to warn Sydney."

"A lot of good the gates and cameras were."

"It was a breach, plain and simple." Nearly bouncing in place, Carlos's excess energy told of his agitation. "Whether there is one guy or two, the whole thing is pretty brazen, what with the police swarming around the grounds."

"We'll need to report this to royal security." William sounded glum. "They won't be happy."

"*I'm* not happy!" Chase exploded. "First the sniper, then this."

Despite her churning stomach, Sydney felt unnaturally calm. "This person, or people, have just upped the threat. They got awfully close this time. Closer than the car trying to run us off the road."

They all stared at her.

"Sydney—" Chase began.

"No. I'm not safe here. They were inside the gate, disabled the cameras, set smoke bombs and shot a poor servant, just because she has the same color hair as me. I need to go somewhere else. Someplace safe."

"They found you here," Jim spoke up. "How do you know they won't find you again if we move you?"

Sydney crossed her arms. "Has anyone thought to wonder *how* they found me?"

Grim-faced, Chase nodded. "I'm afraid there's someone on the inside, communicating your moves. That's the only explanation."

"But who?" Carlos asked.

"We're actively trying to find out. But the fact remains that this person, or people, knows enough about the royal lodge to breach its defenses. This is a problem." He looked at each of them, his expression only softening when he reached Sydney. "And as Carlos said, they're bold as hell. Any ideas, anyone?"

No one spoke at first. Finally, Carlos stepped forward. "I think we need to request extra guards from Silverton if we're going to stay here much longer. I agree with Sydney. This is no longer a safe environment. Personally, I'd recommend we head out."

"I'm inclined to agree with you." Pulling Sydney to him, Chase kept his arm around her shoulders. She didn't even attempt to pull away. Having his strength so close made her feel better, even if it was only temporary.

"You'll need to check with the duke," Jim reminded him.

"I will." Chase's voice was hard. "But no matter what, we need to move Sydney."

The telephone rang, startling them. William answered, listened and then hung up. "At lease we've received one bit of good news. That was the hospital. That woman who was shot has been moved from critical condition to stable. The doctor anticipates a full recovery."

Though Sydney forced a smile, genuinely glad, even that bit of information didn't help dispel her overwhelming foreboding. She had to keep pushing back an edge of panic, wanting to grab her suitcase and her cello and run.

When they exited the security room, she felt even more vulnerable.

As though he sensed this, Chase stayed by her side. But he was clearly distracted, not saying much, waiting for the duke to phone.

Finally, she sent him away with some nonsense about needing to take a nap herself.

But she couldn't go to her room. There she felt trapped. If the killer knew enough about the estate to disable the security cameras without sending out an alarm, they no doubt knew where she slept.

So she drifted around the house like a ghost, staying away from windows, as the day lengthened. Though William, Jim and Carlos watched her, they kept their distance. Restless and frustrated, she wondered if her worries were communicating themselves to her baby. For his or her sake, she hoped not.

Dusk came and she refused to turn on any lights, or allow anyone else to illuminate the rooms she occupied. Eventually, Chase found her, took one look at her face and led her into the room which housed the indoor pool, giving the other men a glare that clearly said they weren't to be disturbed. Pulling the blinds closed on all the windows, he locked the door behind them.

"Did you hear from the duke?"

"Yes. He's got the Lazlo Group working on another safe spot for us."

She nodded. "All of us? Can we plan a way to split up temporarily, so this stalker won't find us?"

"It will be just you and I."

Staring, she studied his shuttered expression. "Why?"

"I don't know who to trust. So you and I will be leaving without telling any of the others."

"I don't know about that. I..."

"I do." He held out his hand. "Come here."

Without a word, she moved into his arms. He kissed the side of her neck and she trembled, wishing she could stop feeling as though she were trying to wake from a long, endless sleep full of nightmares.

"It's going to be all right." He kissed her again, trailing his mouth to her ear, grazing her earlobe before moving along her cheek and finally capturing her lips.

She closed her eyes, swaying against him. Mouth lingering, the gentleness of his kiss challenged her. The slow exploration of his tongue drove her fears from her. Burning...there was only him. She drank him in, welcomed him.

Though his breathing sounded harsh, he undressed her with such reverence that her knees went weak. Standing naked before him, she kept her gaze locked on his, her mouth going dry as he began to remove his own clothing.

Then she went to him. He met her halfway.

They fell onto a nearby chaise longue, pushing away the stack of clean, white towels. The warmth of the heated water, combined with the sharp scent of chlorine were barely noticed, so intent were they on each other.

When he entered her, she shuddered. And when his lips

again claimed hers, she admitted to herself how much he mattered to her. This man, his touch, had become her everything.

The last thought she had before she gave herself over to sensation, was how much she wished they could become a family. Chase, herself and her unborn baby.

Afterwards, Sydney couldn't sleep. Chase didn't seem to have the same problem. At her insistence, they'd remained in the poolroom, bunking down on the cushioned chaises.

Lying beside him listening to his deep, even breathing made her feel even more restless. She eased herself from the chair, standing on shaky legs, and slid into the pool.

The water felt cool and soothing.

Taking a deep breath, she began to swim laps. Maybe if she continued until she could move no more, she might be able to sleep.

The splash of her inelegant breaststroke woke Chase.

"Sydney?" Chase sat up, dragging his hand through his hair. "What's wrong?"

She swam to the side and rested her elbows on the edge. "I'm working off my frustration and fear. How long do you think it'll be before we can leave this place?"

"Tomorrow." His eyes gleaming in the dim light, he rose and slipped into the water next to her. He ran his hands down her side, making her shiver. "You feel good."

"Not inside. I'm scared to death. We've got to get away from here."

He kissed the side of her neck. "I agree. And we will. But not tonight. Carrington's promised to call me first thing in the morning."

She shifted restlessly in his arms. "There's no way I can sleep tonight."

One more kiss, moving from her neck to her lips. This one was long and deep and drugging. When he pulled back, she was breathless.

"Who said anything about sleeping?"

The next morning, the sun streaming in through the poolroom skylights woke them. Despite her worries, Sydney had finally drifted to sleep in Chase's arms.

"Good morning." While he watched, she stretched. He felt a stab of desire. As though they hadn't made love twice in the night, he craved her. He wanted her again, right here, right now.

As he pushed himself to his feet to clear his head, his cell phone rang. Carrington. He glanced at Sydney.

Watching him, she gave a half-awake smile and shrugged. "Go ahead and take your call. I'm going to have a nice hot shower." Blowing him a quick kiss, she climbed out of the chaise. He glimpsed long legs and creamy skin before she slipped out of the poolroom, closing the door behind her.

He flipped open the phone. "Savage here."

"Chase, while I was checking on options for you, I got more bad news," Carrington began without preamble, highly unusual for him. "The Lazlo Group has put Sydney high on their list of suspects in Reginald's murder. That might even be the real reason someone wants to kill her. You might be trying to protect a murderess."

Stunned, Chase froze. He couldn't move, couldn't speak. Though the duke never spoke rashly or without just cause, this time he was way off base. Sydney? No way.

Chase spoke carefully. "What are they basing this on?"

"A woman matching her description was seen with the prince the night he died. She would have had a good reason."

"A good reason? Numerous women are scorned by the men who got them pregnant. That's not reason enough to kill."

"Not reason enough? For killing Reginald? Come on, man. You knew the prince." It was the first time Chase had ever heard Carrington disparage his relative, though all knew there'd been no love lost between them.

"True." Chase had to work on keeping his tone even. "But if she killed Reginald, who's trying to kill her?"

"Who knows? There are hundreds of possible reasons. Maybe she's part of a larger plot. Her country—Naessa itself—could be involved. Maybe someone is trying to silence her so she can never confess."

Chase ran a hand through his hair. "I'm not believing this. Are there any other suspects besides her?"

"The Lazlo Group is looking into numerous leads, including a terrorist cell that might be affiliated with Sheik Kadir Al-Nuri. But right now, more evidence points to Sydney Conner than to anyone else."

Grimly, Chase tried to picture Sydney killing. Doing so was a stretch of the imagination he couldn't quite manage. "No hard evidence though, right?"

"True. It's speculation at this point. But I can promise you we'll get to the bottom of this." Carrington sounded optimistic. "If it *was* her, she'll have made a mistake and they'll find a clue. The Lazlos are good."

They were more than good, they were legendary. In any battle, Chase wanted them on his side. Too bad he couldn't enlist their services to find out who was after Sydney. But they were focused on trying to prove she'd killed the prince.

Sydney a killer. No way. Carrington didn't know her the

way he did. "I know they're good, but they must have more to go on than someone saying they saw her with him. She carries his child. I still don't understand what she'd accomplish by killing him."

There was silence while Carrington considered. That was one thing Chase had always liked about his boss; the duke was not given to rash or impulsive actions.

"Maybe she wasn't thinking clearly," Carrington finally said. "Both Reginald's e-mails and his actions made it clear he wanted nothing to do with her or her baby. You know what they say about a woman scorned. It's possible she went to him, they made love, and she tried one last time to get him to accept responsibility for his actions."

Even now, the mention of Sydney making love with Reginald made Chase wince. "You think when Reginald refused…"

"She decided to kill him."

"That doesn't sound like Sydney. Believe me, I know her. She wouldn't do something like that."

Again the duke fell silent. When he spoke again, his tone was sharp. "Chase, you sound as if you're becoming far too involved with this woman. Last time we spoke, I asked you to be careful."

"I—" Swallowing hard, he bit back any retort. "I'm fine. What about us moving? Have you found us a place?"

Carrington went silent. "I've had a change of heart."

"What?" Chase's heart sank. "What do you mean? She's got to be moved."

"Oh, I agree. But the Lazlo Group wants to question her about the murder."

Chase's pulse began to pound. "What are you saying?"

"I'm ordering you back immediately. With Sydney."

For the first time since starting to work for Carrington, Chase questioned an order. "Sir, with all due respect, I don't think that's a good idea. There's someone working on the inside. If I bring her back to Silvershire, she'll be a sitting duck."

"Bring William and the rest of your men to help you guard her. There's no help for it. We've got to find the prince's killer. If she did it, she's going to prison."

"Sydney Conner is not a killer."

The duke ignored him. "Notify everyone to get ready. The chopper is being dispatched within the hour."

Closing the cell phone, Chase felt numb. All along, he'd asked to be allowed to go back to Silvershire, back in the thick of things, in his element. He'd wanted to be allowed to do his real job, rather than acting as some overblown bodyguard to a pregnant princess.

But that was before he'd come to know Sydney. He couldn't take her back to Silvershire. Protecting her would be damn near impossible. She'd view this as a betrayal. And rightly so, as he'd promised to keep her safe.

Safe. Hell, he didn't even trust his own men. How could he protect her once she was at court?

Yet if he didn't take her back, he'd be allying himself with her, in the duke's eyes. He'd lose his job. Carrington would never forgive him for disobeying a direct order and choosing a possible murderess over him.

Mind in turmoil, he took a deep breath and went down to the gym to work out. Maybe after a good thirty minutes and some well-deserved sweat, he might be able to figure another way out.

When he'd lifted enough weights to make his muscles

ache and pummeled the punching bag until even his teeth hurt, Chase stepped into the shower. How well did he know Sydney, after all? He'd known Kayla a lot better, or so he'd thought, and she'd left him at the altar for another man with more money and a better title.

But this was Sydney. Whether or not they made a future together, her life was in danger. She needed him, perhaps even more as a bodyguard than a mate.

His job had once mattered more to him than anything else, including Sydney Conner. And now? He was no longer certain.

Toweling off, he knew what he had to do. Though he didn't want to admit it, he'd already made a tentative decision.

Now all that remained was one final test.

Chapter 13

Following the sound of childish laughter, Chase found Sydney and Martha in one of the indoor gardens, tossing a brightly colored ball back and forth over the well-tended grass.

As usual, the sight of Sydney made his breath catch in his throat. Skylights provided sunlight, and the golden glow made her creamy skin appear even silkier. She wore shorts and a halter top. For the first time, he detected a bit of roundness in her stomach. Laughing with Martha, intent on tossing the ball, she hadn't noticed him yet.

Watching her play, he felt another kind of ache. Though he'd never been an imaginative man, he thought he might have been given a glimpse five years into the future. She'd frolic with her own child in much the same way, gathering him or her up in a quick hug, before she bestowed a loving kiss.

He wished the baby she carried was his. Stunned, he looked away, before finding his gaze drawn right back to her, waiting for her to see him.

Martha noticed him first, her exuberant smile fading as she took in his serious expression.

"Sydney?"

Her own smile faltering at his tone, she gazed up at him, searching his face with her impossibly blue eyes. "Chase? What's up?"

"I need to talk to you." He kept his voice neutral.

Sydney tilted her head and looked at him, the glorious fire of her hair mussed as though a lover had just run his fingers through it during lovemaking.

His body instantly responded. Damn.

Her sapphire eyes were clear and guileless. "Now?"

"Yes" His gruff tone spoke of his inner turmoil. The chopper would be here shortly. "We don't have much time."

Instantly alert, she nodded. "Let me take Martha back to the kitchen so her aunt can keep an eye on her."

Without a backward glance, she walked over to the little girl, who'd become entranced by a jewel-colored butterfly. She sat with her hand outstretched, the fragile creature perched on her finger, fluttering its brilliant wings.

Chase watched as Sydney bent and spoke quietly to the child, then helped her flutter her tiny fingers, setting the butterfly free. She led Martha by the hand, attempting to skirt Chase, but Martha pulled free and ran barreling at him, throwing herself at his legs so hard he staggered.

"Whoa, there."

She slid to the ground and peered up at him. "My mama says you saved my life."

"Sydney did," he told her, smiling despite his inner turmoil. "I only helped."

"Mama says I should thank you." She blew him a delicate kiss. "Thank you."

Touched, Chase blew her kiss back. "You're welcome. Now go with Miss Conner. She has something she needs to do."

"Something impor…im…portant?" She grinned as she struggled with the word.

"Yes. Very important." Sydney scooped Martha up in her arms, swinging the giggling child high before setting her on her feet. "Let's go, you." She led the little girl off, shooting one last smiling look at Chase over her shoulder.

Chase felt that look in the depths of his stomach. He was in far too deep. That made it even more necessary for him to be absolutely certain.

He'd offer her the check for seven hundred and fifty thousand pounds. If her amazing blue eyes lit up with excitement and she grabbed at the money with a promise to run, he'd know. Then he'd go back to Silverton, to the duke and his job and leave her to her own devices.

If not…he felt dizzy thinking of the possibilities.

Waiting, he paced until she returned.

"Chase?" She walked up to him, still smiling. She'd gathered her unruly hair into a ponytail. He itched again to run his fingers through it, freeing the auburn strands to caress her face and shoulders.

Wincing, he pushed that thought away.

"What's wrong?" She came closer, bringing with her the light floral scent she wore. "Why do you look so grim? What did the duke have to say?"

"I have a lot to tell you in a very short time. He took a

deep, shuddering breath. "First off, they've discovered Reginald didn't die from a cocaine overdose as they'd originally thought."

She frowned. "Cocaine? That's odd. He never used the stuff around me. I'd heard the rumors, of course. But actions speak louder than words, and since I never saw him take, smoke or snort anything, I figured they weren't true."

"They were," he told her, keeping his voice as level as possible. "But that's not what killed him."

She waited, her open expression expectant.

He took a deep breath. "Reginald was murdered. Someone poisoned him."

Sydney reacted exactly as he'd expected, the way an innocent person would. With shock. "Murdered? Why? Who? Are you sure?"

"I'm just repeating what I was told. They don't have a suspect yet." He told the lie casually, still intent on her reaction.

"What about us moving? Where does he want us to go?"

"That's just it. He won't authorize a move." Another lie, but no way was he letting her know he was willing to give up his job for her until he was certain.

She gasped. "Won't authorize a move? But it's not safe here. You know that! What are we supposed to do?"

His heart gave a foolish leap at the way she said *we*. Ruthless, he quashed it. "Sydney, you have a choice. When I found you at the Hotel Royale, I brought a check with me. A certified bank check for seven hundred and fifty thousand pounds."

Crossing her arms, she waited, her expression puzzled.

"I was authorized to offer it to you. They wanted me to offer you the money to disappear, right away."

Silence. She just looked at him. When she finally spoke, he couldn't discern any hint of emotion in her voice.

"Where to?" Her face was blank, her eyes so dark he couldn't read them.

His heartbeat a painful thud in his chest, he took a deep, shuddering breath. "I don't know. America, perhaps? South Africa? Australia? There are several places you could go. All of them far away, all of them much safer."

"So you want me to take your money—excuse me—the crown's money, and make myself and my baby disappear. Do I have that correct?"

"No." He held himself absolutely still, afraid if he moved he'd shatter into a thousand pieces. "That's not what I want. But what I want doesn't matter. This is about you—what do you want to do?"

Again silence, this time stretching out for so long he fought the urge to pace. Or hit something, which had him thinking fleetingly of how badly he needed to make another trip to the gym. A few more rounds with the punching bag might help.

Her gaze searched his face. It wasn't bright, nor expectant, but wounded and hurt. When she finally spoke, her voice was clear and cold. "I'm not willing to do that." She regarded him as if she didn't know him.

He ached to hold her, but knew she wouldn't permit that, not until he explained.

"Sydney, I didn't think you would, but I wanted you to know everything, every option you had available." Quickly he outlined his conversation with Carrington.

She shook her head, the disgust in her voice making him smile. "They really think I killed him?"

"You're a suspect, no more. I know better. You no more

killed Reginald than I did." If he had more time, he could hold her and tell her how he felt. But that would have to come later, once they were safe.

"Hurry and get your things. We've got to go before the chopper gets here. I'll meet you at your room."

"What about William, Carlos and Jim?"

"I don't trust anyone from now on. It's just you and me." Allowing himself one quick kiss, he sent her off with a promise to meet her in ten minutes.

Then he went to gather his own things.

Practically running when she reached her room, Sydney began throwing her clothing into a suitcase. Without even attempting neatness, she stuffed designer shirts and skirts and jeans all together in a wrinkle-inducing blob. Unlike her. But then, her behavior ever since she'd met Chase Savage had been unlike her.

While she packed, she thought about the bribe. Honestly, she was surprised that Silvershire had believed they could buy her off. Had they truly thought she'd take their damn money and gratefully disappear? But then, they didn't know her at all. Didn't know how many times as a child she had wished her own mother would confront Prince Kerwin and demand he acknowledge his daughter. Instead her mother had eagerly taken the money he'd continued to give her, unwilling to rock the boat and endanger her precious silver spoon.

For money, Frances Conner had ensured her daughter would be considered a bastard her entire life.

Though Sydney could do nothing about her child's legitimacy, especially with Reginald dead, she'd never take money from anyone to make herself and her baby disappear. Her child deserved better than that.

Once she'd crammed everything into her suitcase, she slammed the lid, pushing until the locks clicked. Then she turned her attention to her cello. Though she hated to leave her beloved instrument behind, she had no alternative. Carrying a cello would not only identify her to anyone watching, but slow them down. She could only hope they'd return it to her later, after all this was over.

Just in case, she put her hair up into a tight bun and wrapped a gray scarf around her head. Huge dangling earrings and large sunglasses finished her costume.

Surveying herself in the mirror, she managed a smile. She looked nothing like Sydney Conner, cellist with the symphony. She was ready. Chase should be here any minute.

A tap on her door made her smile.

"Come in."

The door swung open. Jim stepped inside.

"Sydney?"

Remembering Chase had said he didn't even trust his own men, she moved in front of her suitcase, blocking it from view. She couldn't do anything about her appearance. Maybe he would just think she was in a weird mood. "Yes, Jim?"

He looked apologetic as he closed the door behind him.

"I'm sorry to have to do this, but they paid me an awful lot of money." Before she could react, he grabbed her and shoved a cloth over her mouth. The sickeningly sweet scent of chloroform was the last thing she knew.

Moving swiftly, Chase tossed his things in his duffel and weighed his options. He'd have no choice but to borrow one of the cars belonging to the estate. After that, he'd take her to his buddy's hunting cabin in the Silver Mountains.

He slung the duffel over his shoulder and headed down

the hall toward Sydney's room. The plush carpet muffled his footsteps. Her door was closed. First he tapped softly. Then, when he got no response, a bit harder.

No answer. Her door remained closed.

He tried the handle. It wouldn't turn. Locked?

Alarmed, he backed away and, giving himself a good start, used his shoulder as a battering ram. The wood gave. He crashed inside.

The room was empty, save for her cello and suitcase. Her second-story window was open. He ran to it, just in time to see a white cargo van pulling away. Below her window, a wide concrete ledge led to the roof over the kitchen, which gently sloped over the storage room.

Damn it! Heart hammering, he spun and ran for the stairs. Taking the steps two at a time, he hurtled toward the front door.

The gates! They were closed and required special equipment to open.

Instead of barreling down the long drive, he reversed direction and headed toward the security room. The gates were controlled remotely from there. Unless Sydney's abductor had a bypass password, they wouldn't open without approval.

If he got there in time, he could stop the van.

Skidding around the corner, he ran into the room in time to see Carlos turning from the console. The screen from the front-gate camera showed only the closed gate. There was no sign of the van.

"What the hell is this?" He stabbed his finger at the screen. "What happened to the camera? Did it show the white van?"

"White van?" Carlos looked up in alarm. "No, it froze up. The security guy went to check on it. He asked me to monitor the rest."

"What about the gate?" Chase barked. "Tell me you didn't open the gate?"

Wide-eyed, Carlos nodded. "I just did, but that was only Jim."

"Jim?"

"He had to run an errand."

Chase couldn't believe his ears. "An errand?" He swore. "Sydney's been abducted."

"Abducted?" Carlos jumped to his feet. "When?"

"Just now. By Jim's white van." He took off running. But by the time he reached the garage, grabbed a set of keys to a powerful little roadster, and roared down the driveway, there was no sign of the van.

First he drove toward the highway. Despite the way the winding curves gave him glimpses of the road ahead, he saw no sign of the van. The wild countryside flashed past, and finally the sign for the highway came into view.

At the entrance ramp to the highway, he pulled a U-turn. Four lanes of traffic zoomed by. If they'd made it onto that, he'd never catch them.

Just in case, he continued on in the other direction, toward town. As he'd expected, the van had disappeared. Along with Sydney and Jim.

When he got back to the lodge, the chopper had arrived. William waited with Carlos and the pilot.

"The duke wants to know what's going on." Carlos looked wild-eyed. "I didn't know what to tell him, so I told him you'd phone him back."

"What about Jim? Has anyone been able to make contact?"

"We tried Jim's cell phone," William told him. "But one of the maids found it in his room. He left it."

"So he's untraceable." Chase ran his hand through his hair. "Where's the security guard who was on duty? I want to review the tapes. Now."

"He's back in the security room."

Before he'd finished speaking, Chase was already headed there. The security guard was waiting.

"What the hell happened?"

"Someone disabled the front-gate cameras."

In no mood for generalities, Chase restrained himself from grabbing the man's shirt. "Disabled how?"

The guard scratched his neck, grimacing. "They've been set to play rather than record. You see it all the time in movies. Someone inserted a tape to run continuously."

"Let's see the others."

But a review of the tapes revealed nothing.

Chase wanted to punch something—anything.

"Maintain control." William handed him a cell phone. "It's the duke. He says we're all supposed to be en route to Silverton."

Biting back a groan, Chase spoke into the phone. "Savage here."

"What on earth is happening down there? Your men couldn't give me a straight answer."

"They've got Sydney."

"Who's got Sydney?" The duke's icy calm grated on Chase's nerves. "Slow down. What are you talking about?"

Trying to speak as concisely as possible, Chase relayed the afternoon's events.

To his shock, the duke didn't believe any of it. "I think you're all jumping to the wrong conclusion. I doubt she's been kidnapped. She must have gotten wind of the investigation and simply taken off."

"No. Jim was the inside guy."

"Jim's been a loyal employee. Like you, he started as a bodyguard."

"I'm aware of that. But someone got to him."

"Has he—or anyone—called and made demands?"

Chase swallowed. "No, that's what worries me. They've been trying all along to kill her."

"I'll alert Interpol. Leave this up to them, they are trained to handle these things."

Chase's heart pumped so hard and so loudly he feared the duke could hear it over the phone lines. While intellectually he understood what Carrington meant, he knew in his heart he couldn't leave finding Sydney up to the pros."

He had too much at stake. She was his everything.

Carrington wasn't finished. "I still need you here. Once Interpol is on the case, I want you to head back to Silvershire."

Even though his boss couldn't see him, Chase shook his head. "I can't leave now. I've got to find Sydney."

"Send William and Carlos. Your assistant quit yesterday. She couldn't handle the pressure. You've got to get back to the office and take control of things. Otherwise, I'm afraid it'll be a public relations disaster."

Once, hearing something like those words would have made Chase ecstatic. Now, all he could think of was Sydney. "I'm sorry, but William will have to head up the office in my absence. He's fully trained and capable."

"But Chase—" Carrington started to protest. Chase cut him off by flipping the cell phone closed.

William waited expectantly and Chase gave him the order to head back to Silverton in his place. Then he motioned to Carlos.

"I need your help. We've got to figure out a way to rescue Sydney, and quickly. Before they decide to kill her."

Carlos grinned, a flash of white teeth. "Just like in the old days, huh, boss?

Wearily, Chase gave a nod. "Except this time the target is much more important."

"Do you want me to involve the local police?"

"Not yet. We'll let Interpol handle all that. Hunt down the usual sources and see what you can learn from them. We've got to discover where they've taken her."

And pray she was still alive when they found out.

Chapter 14

When she woke, squinting in bright fluorescent light, her heart sank as she realized two things. First, she'd been taken captive and second, they hadn't bothered to blindfold or tie her. If they weren't worried about her seeing what they looked like, it could only mean one thing.

They meant to kill her—and her precious baby.

Sitting up slowly, she swallowed against nausea and swung her legs over the side of the—couch? Yes, she'd been placed on a worn and filthy faded orange couch, the like of which even the most needy charity would turn down.

Head pounding, she stood. Her tongue stuck to the roof of her mouth. Trying to swallow, she gagged. Water. She needed water. Unsteadily she staggered to the door—steel?—and tried the handle. It was locked from outside. Wherever she was, she was a prisoner.

The room swirled. Blinking, taking deep breaths, she tried to focus.

Stay calm. Stay cool.

She had to take stock of her surroundings.

The room, which had concrete walls and no windows, resembled a ten-by-ten basement storage room. *Basement* being the key word. Was she being held in someone's home? Not with concrete walls and a steel door. This seemed more likely to be some kind of underground bunker, like a safe house for high-ranking officials. But where?

Her suitcase hadn't come with her—no surprise there. Her purse lay on the cement floor. She unzipped the top, surprised to find the contents intact.

A moment later, she heard the sound of a key fitting into a lock and a deadbolt sliding back. As the door handle turned, she slowly backed away.

Jim entered, face expressionless. Closing the metal door behind him, he used the key to lock it. When he'd finished, he pocketed the key. "Feeling better now?"

She nodded, trying not to stare at the plastic water bottle he held. Seeing where her attention was fixed, he handed it to her.

Though her mouth was dry, she hesitated.

"It's not drugged." He indicated the steel door. "I've no need to drug you now."

Knowing she had no choice but to believe him, she drank greedily, not stopping until she'd drained the bottle. At least her mouth no longer felt full of cotton.

He continued to watch her without speaking.

She stared back, keeping her gaze on him while she placed the empty bottle on the concrete floor.

"Why, Jim? Chase trusted you. Why'd you do this?"

He grimaced, smoothing his hand over the top of his gray crew cut. "Money, why else? I'm not getting any younger."

"You sold out your government so you could retire?"

His eyes narrowed. "No. You're Naessan. Agreeing to kidnap you has nothing to do with my government."

"Does the duke know you've done this?"

"Of course not." Scorn rang in his voice. "He's an honest man."

And you're not. But she held her tongue, asking instead, "Was it you all along trying to kill me?"

"No. There is more than one faction involved. I was hired to get you out of the line of fire. I came late into the game. Consider yourself lucky," he told her.

"Lucky?"

"Yes. I was told originally one group hired someone to kill you. But he couldn't seem to do the job. He was behind the shootings at the hotel, blowing up your rental car, the car that tried to run your limo off the cliff and the smoke bombs."

"Told by who?"

He didn't answer, merely smiling.

"The jet crashing, too? Did this nameless someone cause that?" She couldn't keep the sarcasm from her voice.

"Unfortunately for him, no. No one knew you'd be on that jet, though if you'd died in the crash it certainly would have simplified things for him. I've been told he even tried to get to you after the crash, before you could be rescued, but the royal chopper beat him to it."

"On that island? How'd he know about that?" She swallowed, refusing to look away. "For that matter, how did he always know exactly where I was, if there wasn't a man on the inside? No matter where I went, he always found me."

He laughed, reminding her with a sharp pang that this was Jim. Jim, who'd always been the quietest member of Chase's team, the consummate grandfather, a family man.

Damn.

Casting a meaningful look at her purse, he held out his hand. "Let me see your purse and I'll show you."

For a moment she stared at him. Finally, she handed it over.

Once he had the black Fendi in his hands, he set it down next to him and pulled a switchblade from his pocket.

Sydney winced out of reflex, making him grin.

"This blade isn't for you. I'm using it to do this." Turning her purse over, he used the sharp knifepoint to pick at the bottom seam. Prying apart a small opening, he used the tips of his fingers and pulled out a tiny, silver disc and held it up. "See?"

She went closer, trying to see. "It's a—"

"Remote tracking device." His grin spread. "This wonderful device is how we knew where you were every second of every day."

A bug. She suppressed the urge to rub her eyes. She felt like an actor in a James Bond movie. "How was that put in my purse? And when? I never let it out of my sight."

"When you perform with the symphony you do. An operative broke into your locker when you were playing in Silverton."

Right about the time she'd started dating Reginald.

"Why? Was it because I was dating the prince?"

He shrugged. "I don't think so. Remember I said there were different factions involved? The first group, the one that wanted to kill you, threatened your father. They tried to use you against him."

"My father?" Dazed, she rubbed her temples. "I don't have a father."

"Really?" Lifting a brow, he wagged a finger at her. "Prince Kerwin would be disappointed to hear that. He saved your life."

"Prince Kerwin?" This was getting stranger and stranger. "He's the mysterious person you keep mentioning? You work for him?"

"Yes. When the first group tried to have you killed, he took care of their hired assassin."

"Took care of how?" She hoped the effects of the chloroform would begin to wear off soon. "What happened to the assassin?"

He shook his head. "In order to gain control of the situation, he eliminated your would-be killer. Right after that maid got shot instead of you."

Eliminated. She swayed, forcing herself to stay focused on his face. She didn't want to know how, or by whom. "And then you were hired by Prince Kerwin? To do what, kidnap me?"

"I was recruited to do exactly that."

"Why?" She crossed her arms. The man who'd sired her had never wanted anything to do with her before. Other than setting up her trust fund, he'd never even attempted to make contact. Why now, and in such a way?

"He hired me to bring you here, get you out of the clutches of the Silvershire people. He didn't want you under their influence until he had time to make an offer."

"Politics?" Her head swimming from more than the chloroform, she tried to make sense of his words. "Now you've really got me confused. You're telling me I was brought here for political reasons?"

He shrugged. "I'm only the messenger."

"But this makes no sense. Politically, I'm worthless. I have no status, no rank, no pull. I'm not worth anything to anyone."

"Ah, but you are more valuable than you realize. Your father is Naessan royalty. And, as an added bonus, you carry the only blood heir to Silvershire's throne. If the people can be convinced that your child must be made next in line for the throne… An explosive combination."

"Illegitimate," she pointed out. Whether she spoke of herself or of her baby, she wasn't sure. Right now, hand cradling her slightly rounded belly, they were one and the same. "The duke will rule in place of Reginald. Royalty never puts a bastard on the throne, you know that."

"Perhaps not in the past. But your father feels that can be changed. Recognized officially or not, you are Prince Kerwin of Naessa's daughter." He waved a hand. "And as far as the baby you carry, whether you and Prince Reginald married or not is irrelevant. Your child is his only known issue. Your child is heir to Silvershire."

Openmouthed, she stared. Jim's eyes burned. He actually believed this nonsense. Fervently. And if he did, others might, as well.

Oh, for the love of… This was ridiculous!

For her baby's sake, she had to figure out a way to make this work to her advantage. She bit her lip. She needed to keep her mouth shut and quit giving them reasons to kill her.

Deep breath. Shoulders back. "Where are we?"

"On Chawder Island."

"Where the jet crashed?" Again he'd succeeded in shocking her. "How is that possible?"

"One of your father's corporations owns this island. After you were rescued, Prince Kerwin opened up this re-inforced, underground bunker he had built years ago."

"Bunker? How is that possible? This island isn't that large. You shouldn't be able to dig very far before hitting water."

"Volcanic rock. Surely you noticed that when you were here before? This little mountain used to be a volcano. Your father explored here and found caves. That led to this bunker."

As though he suddenly remembered whose money lined his pockets, his smile disappeared. "Your father will be here soon. He wishes to make his offer in person."

"And you? What do you get out of this?"

"Besides money?" He took a step closer, still smiling. "I will have the honor of knowing I indirectly saved the future king of Silvershire."

"But the money's more important, right?" At his nod, she took a deep breath, then changed tactics. "How much is he paying you?"

He chuckled. "More than my salary after working ten years for the PR department."

"I'll pay you more."

Shaking his head, he sighed. "Sydney, look. I like you. While I know you have a trust fund, I read the papers. I know you only get two hundred and fifty thousand a year, plus what you earn playing for the symphony. The amount Prince Kerwin offered me is more than you could afford."

Maybe, if she only dipped into her savings. But Chase had offered her seven hundred and fifty thousand. If she could convince him to send it to her...

"Don't bet on that."

He raised one graying brow. "Your father is paying me half a million pounds. Tell me you can beat that."

"I think I might. What if I can give you seven hundred and fifty?"

"Interesting." He frowned. "I don't know. If Prince Kerwin were to find out, I'd be dead. Your father is not a forgiving man."

Steady. "He'll never know. All you'll have to do is say I've escaped."

Jim dragged his hand across his mouth. "I'll have to think about it."

She made an effort to shrug, as though her heart wasn't racing. "Don't think too long. I'll need to make a phone call to get the money here. I want to get away before Prince Kerwin arrives."

"Why?" His gaze bright with interest, Jim stared at her.

"Because my father has never cared about me. Ever. Once he's here, I honestly think he'll kill me himself, so no one can ever threaten to use me against him again."

Without another word, Jim let himself out. Sydney glanced at the filthy couch and looked for somewhere else to sit. She settled on the concrete floor, back to the wall, facing the door. If Jim took her offer, everything would depend on Chase.

Barely half an hour had elapsed before Jim returned.

"I'm taking the seven-fifty," he announced. "Now who do you have to call?"

She kept her face expressionless. "Chase. He has the money. It was given to him by the duke to buy me off."

"Chase?" Jim's face reflected his disbelief. "I'd rather not deal with him."

"You won't have to. I'll call him."

"That's not what I mean." Panic glinted in his eyes. "You don't know Chase."

"He'll pay it." She spoke with more confidence than she felt. She *thought* he'd pay to save her, but the money actually belonged to the Crown. And, ever since Reginald, she no longer trusted her judgment where men were concerned.

"Oh, I know he'll pay. That's not what I mean. After I get paid, I'd planned on taking the money and then disappearing, maybe to a Caribbean island someplace. But not if Chase is involved. No one messes with people he cares about. He'll hunt me down."

A lump stuck in her throat. "That's assuming he cares about me."

"He does." Jim sounded certain. "You forget I was around the two of you. I've seen the way he looks at you."

Sydney tried to look positive, too. Ironic that the fate of her and her baby now rested on the head of royal PR. What a field day the papers would have with that!

"I'll make him promise to leave you alone." She needed to hear his voice. "Are you going to let me call him?"

"No. I'm making the call. That way there's no funny business. But—" his smile seemed overly bright "—he's probably going to insist you talk with him, to prove you're alive. I am going to ask him to give his word to leave me alone. Chase never goes back on his word."

He stared at her a moment longer. "You can't mention Prince Kerwin or the deal's off. Understood?"

"Yes." She had no choice. Nor did she much care. All she wanted was to get herself and her baby out of here alive.

Studying her, he seemed about to ask her something else. But instead, he drew a cell phone out of his pocket. "Then let's give him a call."

* * *

When his cell phone rang, Chase almost missed it. He'd just turned on the shower and was preparing to step into it.

Picking up the phone, his heartbeat skipped. The caller ID showed unknown caller. It had to be Jim with a new cell phone.

"Speak to me, Jim. What have you done with Sydney?"

"She's here. Safe. She tells me you have quite a bit of money on you."

The ransom demand. Every nerve stilled. "Money?"

"The seven hundred and fifty thousand." Jim spoke quietly, as if he was embarrassed.

"Jim, why are you doing this? You've worked with me a long time, going back to when we were both royal bodyguards."

The line went silent. Finally, Jim cleared his throat. "I have Sydney. Do you have the cash or not?"

"It's a bank check—certified. As good as cash." He took a deep breath. "What about Sydney? Is she alive? Unharmed?"

"She's fine."

"Put her on the line."

"No can do. Not yet. Not until you commit to pay."

"I'll pay. If she's all right." Grimly, he contemplated what he'd do to his former employee if he so much as harmed one hair on Sydney's head.

"Give me your word."

"If she's returned to me unharmed, I'll pay. You have my word."

"I also want your word that you won't come after me later, once you have her."

Chase clenched his jaw. He wanted to rip the man apart

with his bare hands. "You have my word," he ground out. "I won't come after you."

"Ever?"

Chase swore. "Ever."

"Good enough. I know you keep your promises." Jim sounded cheerful. "I'll put her on the line."

"Chase?" When Chase heard Sydney's shaky voice, he felt some of the crushing weight lift from his chest. At least in this, Jim hadn't lied. She was still alive. Thank God.

"Sydney, are you all right? You're not hurt, are you?"

"No." He could hear her licking her lips, as though trying to get moisture into her mouth. "I'm not hurt."

"Where are you?"

"Chawder Island, he said. The place where we were—"

"I know." He bit back an oath. "Sydney, listen to me. We've got to—"

"Got to do what?" Jim was back on the line. "Chase, you'd better listen. For the first time in a long time, you're not calling the shots. Here's what I want you to do…"

After Jim concluded the call, he went to the door with the phone still in hand. "Looks like you're going to have to stay locked up a bit longer." He sounded apologetic, as though none of this was his doing. "I don't know how long it'll take him to get here."

"Have you heard from Prince Kerwin?"

"Not yet. We have a little time. He's been busy. I've seen him on the telly. He had to attend some kind of a summit in Tice. Dignitaries from all over the place are there." He smiled at her. Sydney couldn't believe she'd once seen his smile as kind.

"When that's finished, I imagine he'll head out here."

Still smiling, he left, closing the steel door behind him. A moment later, she heard the sound of the dead bolt sliding into place.

Time crawled by. How much time, she couldn't say, since she had no watch. She paced, she raged, she tried to think.

She walked the confines of her cell until her legs hurt. Then, sitting on the edge of her mattress, she examined her perfectly manicured fingernails and sighed. One by one she began methodically picking at the cuticle.

Jim brought her food and she ate it, judging the time of day by what he brought. Since the first meal he brought her was an undercooked piece of chicken and beans, she judged that was her supper. She slept a little, though the cold concrete floor was so uncomfortable, she finally made herself move to the couch.

For breakfast, Jim brought a tasteless porridge, for lunch, runny soup.

When she heard the sound of the dead bolt moving, she guessed it was dinnertime again. But Jim entered the room without a tray, wild-eyed, his shirt half buttoned, as though he'd dressed in a hurry.

"We've got a problem." Clearly agitated, he couldn't stand still. "Prince Kerwin's chopper has radioed they should be landing soon. They'll be here within half an hour."

Sydney closed her eyes. When she opened them, she swallowed. "What about Chase?"

"I don't know. He said he'd be here. But he thinks we've got plenty of time."

Her heart stopped. *Where was Chase?* "What are we going to do?"

He shrugged. "You're going to have to meet with your

father. If Chase shows up afterwards, we can still make it look like you've escaped. This might even work out better."

As the door closed behind Jim, Sydney felt chilled. For the very first time in her life, she was about to meet the man who'd sired her. Once, hearing this news would have been the answer to a little girl's lonely prayers. But now, Prince Kerwin's desire to meet with her had come far too late and was for all the wrong reasons.

He'd never even visited the home she'd shared with her mother, preferring to meet Frances Conner somewhere else to avoid having to see his by-blow.

Did he truly think she'd greet him with open arms? That little girl had grown up long ago.

Yet, when the door of her cell swung open and a tall, silver-haired man dressed in a Gucci suit strode in, her heart still caught in her throat.

Prince Kerwin.

Though she'd seen his face on television and in newspapers, none of that had prepared her for the sheer force of his commanding presence. She tried to breathe normally, act nonchalant, yet found herself wishing for a mirror to ensure she'd pass muster. Dumb. The man she refused to call Father looked, with his broad shoulders and arrogant profile, every inch the royal prince. Silver hair graced his temples, and the cut of his expensive suit flattered his trim body. One brilliant, square-cut diamond flashed from his right pinky.

Oddly enough, he brought Reginald to mind.

A conqueror viewing the vanquished, he entered the room alone, surprising her. She'd expected him to arrive surrounded by bodyguards. No doubt his men waited just outside her cell door. After all, how much damage could an unarmed pregnant woman inflict?

Behind him, framed in the doorway, Jim flashed her a nervous smile before pulling on the heavy steel door. It swung closed behind him with a clang, leaving Sydney and her sire alone.

From across the room, they stared at each other.

"Hello, Sydney." His deep voice sounded warm.

Unable to help herself, she studied his face. She saw her own chin and nose when she looked at him. She'd also gotten her blue eyes from him, but little else. He was tall and lean, while she made up in curves what she lacked in height. He looked royal, while she...was as ordinary as could be. Her best feature was her flame-red hair.

She started to speak and found she couldn't. Her throat felt tight, closed. Odd how meeting him still made her want to cry. Even now, with all he'd done and all he'd refused to do.

Finally, she cleared her throat. "Prince Kerwin."

"I've wanted for years to meet my daughter."

Startled, her gaze flew to his. "You've wanted?" She couldn't keep the bitterness out of her voice. "For years I've longed for a father, but you never once came or called. I even worked up the nerve to ask mother why you didn't want me." She blinked, refusing to cry in front of him.

"And your mother? What did she say?"

Her mother had merely laughed, her cold gaze raking over Sydney in a way that left no doubt she was lacking.

"Sydney?"

"She didn't really answer." She shifted her weight from one foot to the other. "What does it matter? You've never had anything to do with me in the past."

He looked surprised and—unexpectedly—hurt. "Your mother said you both wanted it that way. I paid for everything, and stayed out of the picture. She'd only let me visit the house when you were away at school. Otherwise, we met at a flat I kept in town."

Sydney could only stare, her ears roaring. Was this another trick? Or truth? Had her mother stooped so low as to deny her child her own father? To what end?

So as not to take attention away from herself.

Her mother hadn't wanted to share the prince with anyone, not even their little girl.

Not knowing what to believe, Sydney slowly shook her head. "My mother—Frances—told you that?"

A frown creased his brow. He took a step closer. "Of course. Otherwise I would have made an effort to get to know you. You *are* my daughter, after all. She told you you wanted a quiet life, that I would disturb you."

Either her mother had sunk to new depths of selfish narcissism, or Prince Kerwin was a bold-faced liar. She was betting the actual truth was a combination of both things. "She said you didn't want me."

They stared at each other from identical blue eyes. Finally, he dragged his hand through his perfectly groomed hair. "I should find it no surprise to learn your mother lied to me all these years."

Sydney shrugged. She hadn't spoken to Frances in eighteen months.

The tall, silver-haired man watched her. She couldn't tell if that was sorrow darkening his eyes, or if he was playing her the same way her mother had supposedly played him.

When she didn't answer, he sighed.

He came closer, bringing with him a whiff of expensive cologne. "Haven't you dreamt of having it all? Living at the palace, being part of the court? The luxury, the prestige, the respect—all you've ever wanted, can be yours at the snap of my fingers."

Without thinking, she blurted the truth. "All I ever wanted was your love."

After a moment of silence, while he studied her as if she were a specimen under a microscope, he laughed. And laughed longer, a rich, masculine sound that brought sudden tears springing to her eyes. His laughter mocked her, ridiculed her the same way her mother always had.

Who was she to think such a man could ever love her?

She wanted to shrink back inside herself, to rebuild her protective shell, but her pride wouldn't let her.

"Come now." He grinned at her. "You're as good an actress as your mother. I promise I will make this worth your while."

Actress? If only he knew. Once she would have traded all her toys for a smile from this man.

She drew herself up and looked him straight in the eye. "Do not ever insult me by comparing me with my mother."

Sobering, he nodded. Something must have shown in her face, telling him he'd gone too far. "It's not too late. We can change things." His warm smile invited her to come closer.

Now, she knew he wanted only to use her. He didn't really care about establishing a relationship or getting to know her.

It shouldn't have hurt, but it did. More than she'd expected.

She wanted to tell him to go straight to hell.

But she couldn't. Provoking him might only make him decide to finish what the assassins had started. She had to stall for time until Chase could get there and she could escape. She no longer had only herself to think of. She had her unborn child to protect.

Chapter 15

"With all due respect, Prince Kerwin, let's dispense with the lies. I'm aware that you couldn't care less about me." She hoped she wouldn't gag on the next words. "Your offer interests me. What do you want from me in exchange?"

He smiled approvingly. "I knew you were your moth—"

She shot him a glare of warning.

"All right, then. How much do you know? I'm sure Jim explained everything to you." He reminded her of Reginald at his most arrogant.

"Not everything. I know you were going to have me killed." Carefully, she watched for his reaction.

"Not I." He looked offended. "I saved your life. My colleagues would have preferred you were permanently out of the way. I had their hired gun removed."

"Why?" Though Jim had already told her, she wanted to hear her sire answer in his own words.

"You can be more useful to me alive than dead. I have great plans for you."

She crossed her arms, hugging herself. "Plans? Could you be more specific?"

Obviously, Prince Kerwin wasn't used to being questioned. He looked down the length of his aristocratic nose at her, brows raised. "Honestly, didn't your mother teach you anything? My plans are not your concern."

"Ah, but they are," she told him, her voice as silky-smooth as his had been earlier. "If you want me to stand firmly on your side, tell me what you're planning."

Again he glared at her in ringing silence. Motionless, Sydney waited him out.

Finally, he sighed again. "Now that Silvershire is without an heir, I think the people will accept your child. Once you ally yourself—and your precious child—with me, we will choose you a husband." His laughter had a sharp edge. "I'm involved in negotiations with two neighboring countries, Besel and Leandra. Both the kings have sons of marriageable age. Once you marry one of them, your child will speak for the combined countries."

"They'd marry me, knowing I carry another man's baby?"

He laughed, the sound sharp. "Don't you understand? Your unborn child is the key. Joined with you, your husband's country will gain a great deal of power. Naessa will no longer stand alone against Silvershire."

"And what of Silvershire?" she asked softly, cradling her slightly rounded belly.

His eyes gleamed. "Silvershire will no longer be the only powerful nation. Naessa will also have that status, under my guidance and leadership."

"Shouldn't that come from within the country first? We are a small nation, without a large army or—"

"Of course." He cut her off. "I plan to expand Naessa. My father doesn't have much faith in my ability to lead. This will prove him wrong."

King Charles had to be eighty, at least. "So you act without the throne's authority in this?"

He narrowed his eyes. "They will back me, once it becomes obvious I can win. That's where you come in. You and your wonderful, doubly royal baby. Heir to the crown of Silvershire. What better way to sway the people to my side?"

She could only stare. For so long she'd dreamed of meeting this man and now…he made her skin crawl.

"When you talk about expanding Naessa, are you thinking of starting a war with Silvershire?"

He didn't even blink. "If that's what it takes. Silvershire has grown complacent. I'm working with various allies, in secret of course, to gather an army. With you on my side carrying the heir to their crown, bloodshed might not be necessary."

Like any good politician, he'd put the ball squarely back in her court. "You're saying if I don't agree with you, people will die?"

"Perhaps."

Another horrible thought occurred to her. "Speaking of dying, did you kill Reginald?"

For the first time, she managed to startle him. "No. Quite honestly, I was planning to buy him off. If he'd lived, he would have made a perfect puppet. With his excesses and low moral fiber, he would have done anything for money."

How could he, with his plots and secret plans, talk about someone else's low moral fiber?

Something of her thoughts must have shown in her face. He flashed an arrogant smile that told her he didn't care.

"Think about my offer. Join forces with me. Proclaim to the world that you and the next heir to Silvershire will be aligned with Naessa, plus the country of whichever prince you marry."

"And if I don't?"

"If you don't?" He gestured at the concrete walls. "I could have you killed now, but I won't."

"You'd let me go?" She couldn't believe it. "Just like that, you'd let me go free?"

His expression went cold, remote. "That's not what I said, Sydney. You know too much to let you live. I will keep you here, a prisoner, until the baby is born. As far as the world will know, you will have died in childbirth. In truth, I'll order my men to kill you."

So much for fatherly love. Compressing her lips into a tight line, Sydney stood motionless, expressionless, and watched the man she would never call Father take his leave.

Take his offer or die. Not much of a choice. Unless…for the first time in her life, Sydney knew she'd have to think and act just like her enemies. That was her only hope—to pretend to go along with their plans, and hope she could warn Chase in time.

Even if Prince Kerwin paid Jim the money he wanted, no doubt he had a small army camped outside. Trying to help her escape, Chase could get killed. Now she not only had to worry about the safety of her unborn child, but also the man she loved.

Chase bailed out over the ocean at night, at thirty-five hundred feet. The plane—one of the new, superquiet, superlight aircraft built specifically for the Silvershire air force—sped silently away.

Because he was jumping from so low an altitude, he immediately pulled his ripcord, feeling the swift, sharp pull upward as his parachute billowed into the pitch-black sky. His knapsack contained night-vision goggles and, of course, the certified bank check for seven hundred and fifty thousand pounds.

Drifting toward the beach, he came in on the opposite side of the island from where the jet had crashed, away from the shadow of the mountain where he and Sydney had nearly made love for the first time and where, according to Jim's instructions, he was to bring the money.

No longer bribe money, the check had become blood money. He planned on turning over none of it. Not one red cent. Instead, he meant to free Sydney and bring troops swooping down on the island.

He only hoped he wasn't too late.

Chase had come an awfully long way, taken a huge risk, and enlisted the help of Silvershire's military forces, all on his gut instinct. Things were bigger than they seemed. Whoever had paid Jim would come eventually, and he wanted to catch the bigger fish as well as the small.

Most importantly, he wanted to find Sydney.

The landing was soft and good, and the lack of a breeze kept the parachute from carrying him too far down the beach. Dragging his parachute into the underbrush, he slipped on the night-vision goggles. He moved silently and kept to the forest as he made his way to the mountain.

A sound made him freeze. Damn—that could only be the sound of a low-flying chopper approaching.

It flew over him, heading toward the mountain.

In the morning he was supposed to meet with Jim at the base of the mountain to exchange the money.

Who was in the chopper? Jim and Sydney? Or was it the one behind Jim's defection, the one in charge?

He supposed he'd find out in the morning.

Before then, he'd do a bit of recon work and see what else he could discover.

For a good while the only sounds he heard were the normal, night sounds of the forest. Small animals moved about in search of food, but he was the only human.

So far so good. He kept his steady path toward the small mountain. A few minutes later, he heard the faint hum of man-made machinery. Jeeps and generators, several men. Jim's associates?

Circling around the pond, he kept going. He remained in the shadows as he drew closer. A dog barked and he froze, only cautiously moving forward when it was quiet again.

There was some sort of camp at the base of the mountain. Careful to make no sound, he peered through the foliage to take a head count.

There were only a few men, less than he'd expected. He counted three, before a fourth emerged from a tent, whistling as he walked. All soldiers in camouflage. All armed to the teeth. They were camped around a door that had been cut into the side of the mountain.

A door? He'd climbed this mountain when he and Sydney had been trapped here before, done his share of exploring, but hadn't noticed the door. How had he missed it and where did it lead? Underground bunkers? Then he saw the elaborate screen they used to cover everything and understood why the place had gone undetected. Once the screen was in place, covered as it was with leaves and dirt and rocks, no one would ever find the door.

What kind of covert operation had captured Sydney?

A second later, he had his answer. A royal one. The helicopter he'd heard earlier sat on a well-lit landing pad built at the edge of the beach. The sides were painted with the royal crest of Naessa. Two large German shepherds were chained to stakes near the helicopter. He recognized the dogs from television. They were Prince Kerwin's pets and traveled everywhere with him.

Prince Kerwin. That explained the soldiers and the underground bunkers. Naessa might be small, but it was a wealthy country.

So why the phone call from Jim demanding money? And how was Sydney involved? Her birth father was Prince Kerwin. This brought more questions he couldn't answer.

He couldn't help but wonder if he'd blundered into some kind of trap. Since he had no choice, he supposed it didn't really matter.

For now. Once the military got here, there'd be answers, he guaranteed it.

Now, before anything else, he'd need to focus on the most important question of all. Where was Sydney being held and how was he going to get to her?

After he got her out, he was home free. One press of the button he wore on his belt, and the transmitter would send a prearranged signal. Silvershire Special Forces would swoop down on the island and secure it. But until he found Sydney, he worked alone.

He hunkered down to wait and plan.

Flanked by two burly bodyguards, Sydney followed Prince Kerwin down the long hall. At each corner, the incline became more and more steep.

"I had this underground bunker designed incorporating several natural caves. This path will gradually emerge on the surface," the prince said, expansive now that he thought he had another fan. "Masterpiece of a hiding place, don't you think?"

Was it ever. "I can't believe we didn't find any signs of this place when we were trapped here."

"Ah yes, you and that man." They turned another corner. "Your fiancé? What became of him?"

As she struggled to find an answer, the lights went out, plunging them into darkness.

Though she was as surprised as the rest of them, Sydney knew an opportunity when she saw one. Spinning past her bodyguards, she elbowed one in the gut. The other one grabbed her arm, so she kicked him, her toe connecting with his soft parts. Grunting in pain, he let her go.

She ran like hell in the pitch-black hallway, up, always up, heading toward the exit. Slamming into walls, careening off corners, bruised and battered but always protecting her abdomen, she kept ahead of the furious prince and his guard.

Then, rounding another turn in the darkness, she realized she could see her hands. Ahead of her she saw light. Outside! She was that close!

As she barreled into a holding room that led to the main hallway, the way looked miraculously clear.

A few more feet and she'd have her freedom.

A shape loomed up in front of her. Big, bulky. A man. Crap! She attempted to dodge. He grabbed her arms.

No. With an inarticulate sound of rage, she fought him.

"Sydney, stop." Chase's voice. She froze, long enough to focus on his face. Chase. Here. She didn't have time to wonder how or why. It was enough that he was.

"Run," she managed, pushing away an unbelievable swell of joy. "No time to explain. They'll be up here any minute."

Two men lay on the ground, face down.

"I took them out. Come on."

They sprinted, running side by side, crashing full speed into the forest. Without stopping they rushed, jumping over the occasional fallen log, pushing aside the undergrowth, and hoping like hell the dogs weren't released.

When they reached the deepest part of the woods, a good distance from the camp, they rested. Doubled over, Sydney tried to listen for sounds of pursuit. She heard nothing.

Chase bent over next to her. "Until they send the dogs after us, we're okay. I disabled the four guys outside."

Trying to catch her breath, Sydney gasped for air. "Dead?"

"No. Unconscious."

"Good." She frowned. "Chase, I haven't seen Jim."

He shook his head. "We'll deal with him later. Silver-shire troops will be here soon. I've sent them a signal. We've got to keep going."

"Where?"

The sound of dogs barking carried through the trees.

"Damn!" Chase jumped to his feet. "The only place dogs can't track us is water. Come on, we're going to have to go back to the pond. Remember I told you about the underwater route to the hidden caves I found?"

She nodded.

"Let's go."

Though exhaustion had her stumbling, Sydney pushed herself up.

As they drew nearer the pond, the sound of barking and baying grew louder. Chase wondered how many dogs they were using in the search. No matter. Water would stop the dogs from going any further. Unless their pursuers knew about the hidden cave, they'd be safe until reinforcements arrived. Until then, they needed to hide.

More than anything, Chase wanted to keep Sydney safe.

Finally, they reached the pond and waded in together to their knees. After a quick look at Sydney, Chase held out his hand. She took it without hesitation, allowing him to pull her chest-high into the murky water.

"Once we're under, open your eyes and follow me. I did this when we were here before. There's a rock wall that leads to the caves on the right. We'll follow that and, just when you think you can't hold your breath any longer, we'll surface in an underground cave. It's like a huge air bubble. There's a ledge and a couple of other flat places to climb, which we'll need to do to get out of the water. We're going to hide in the cave for a little while. Are you ready?"

She swallowed and nodded.

He pressed a quick kiss to her lips and then, releasing her, he waited while she dove in. A second later, he followed.

The rock wall was exactly as he remembered and, lungs bursting, he felt his way quickly along the smooth surface. Sydney was right with him. Then, when the rock abruptly ended, he grabbed her arm and pushed them both up the craggy face of the ledge.

As he'd done the first time he'd tried this, he wondered if he was going to make it. Then, miraculously, they popped out of the water, gasping for air.

He held on to the rock face with one hand, Sydney with the other. "Are you all right?"

Still trying to pull oxygen into her lungs, she nodded. "I think so."

Hauling himself up on the ledge, he reached for her.

Shaking her head, she pulled herself up. They rested a moment, before climbing the rest of the way.

As they reached the small cave, she was shivering. Chase pulled her close, holding her.

God, she felt good wrapped in his arms once more. Where she belonged.

He nuzzled her wet hair. She raised her face to his, a question in her eyes. "What are we going to do?"

"Wait here until help arrives."

Sydney seemed to accept this answer, relaxing slightly. Somehow, despite all she'd been through, she still managed to look sleekly pampered. And, he admitted to himself, sexy as hell.

"When'd you get here?"

He smiled. "Last night. Right about the same time Prince Kerwin did. Now tell me what's going on."

She filled him in. Once she'd finished, Chase gave a low whistle. "Talk about convoluted. And the sad part about it is he was right about Reginald. I know how you felt about him, but Reginald would have sold out his country for a good time."

"How I felt about him?" Twisting her hands in her lap, she sighed. "I realize now I never really knew Reginald. I heard the stories, of course. But he was different with me. Right up until he ended it, he acted as if I'd changed him, made a difference."

He kissed her, hard. "You probably did, for a while."

"Maybe. But I know now I never really knew him. Nor he me."

Chase had to know. "What about the baby, Sydney?"

"He and I never discussed the baby, after the first time. Once I told him I was pregnant, as far as he was concerned

I didn't exist. He wouldn't see me. He ignored my e-mails and refused to take my calls. He pretended not to know me."

Again, Chase found himself wondering at Reginald's monumental stupidity. To have had the love of a woman like Sydney, and then to discard it....

His own thoughts struck him like a sledgehammer.

Love. He pushed the thought away for later.

"So, what do you think?" He gestured around them. "Even though they can't be reached by land, the tops of these caves are above ground. See all the light? There must be some small holes somewhere."

Taking in their surroundings, she smiled. "Pretty neat. I've never been caving."

"As caves go, it's not much. But it's hidden, safe and dry. We can hang out here until we know the island has been secured."

She pressed against her stomach. "How long?"

"As long as it takes."

"Without food or water?"

"The pond water is safe to drink. I've tried it. Worst comes to worst, we can go a day or so without food."

She nodded, though she looked so uncertain he couldn't resist kissing the side of her neck, making her shiver.

"I'm worried about my baby."

He drew back and turned her chin to face him. "Did anyone hurt you?"

"No, it's not that. I have to make sure I'm getting enough nutrients. I don't have my vitamins or—"

He covered her mouth with his. This time, he deepened the kiss and she sagged against him. When he lifted his mouth, she sighed. "I can't help worrying, Chase."

"We'll be fine," he told her, aching for more than a kiss.

He never wanted to be parted from her again, though now wasn't the time to tell her that.

"Yes, I'm sure we will be." Pushing herself out of his arms she stood and wrapped her own arms around herself. She sounded strong as she met his gaze, her own determined.

"Anything's better than being a prisoner in that underground concrete bunker of theirs."

To distract himself, he fished a plastic bag from his pocket. "Waterproof," he said, breaking the seal. "This is the transmitting device I told you about. I've activated the signal, so it's only a matter of time."

Shaking her head, Sydney laughed. "Shades of James Bond, eh?"

"Maybe." He grinned back.

"Silvershire has a hell of a PR department. What's up with that?"

"We're prepared for anything." He placed the small metal box on a nearby rock ledge. "Not only do we protect the royal reputations, but we are all trained to protect their lives, as well. Some of us are former bodyguards, like William, Carlos and Jim." He clenched his jaw, wondering how the man he'd known for years had come to betray him.

"Chase?" Sydney came back to Chase's side. "We need to talk."

Before, in any of his previous relationships, those four words had inspired dread. But this was Sydney, and Chase merely nodded and pulled her into his lap.

"Come here."

Breathless, she put up a mock struggle. "I said talk, not cuddle." But still, she let him pull her close, settling nicely in his lap. Heaving a sigh, she leaned her head on his shoulder.

"I've missed you," he told her. Holding Sydney, he realized he never wanted to let her go.

They spent the remainder of that night wrapped in each other's arms. At first, he checked his watch every hour. Then, as Sydney dozed, he finally fell asleep.

When he woke, he saw it was seven in the morning.

Gently easing Sydney out of his arms, he stood and stretched, working out the kinks in his body. When he looked at her again, he saw she was awake, and watching him.

They shared some water and some of his military rations.

Fidgety, he tried to pace. The small confines made this difficult. He did it anyway.

She exercised. Sit-ups, push-ups, jumping jacks. He thought about joining her, but settled back to watch instead.

Finally, he couldn't take the silence. "They should be here by now. I'm going to go check."

"Out there? Do you think it's safe?"

He touched her arm. "We won't know until I find out. We can't stay here forever."

She nodded. "I'm going with you then."

"No. Let me—"

"Hey." She pressed her nose against his, making a mock growling sound. "Don't mess with a hungry pregnant woman. I'm going for the food."

"No. The baby's better off away from bullets. You wait here."

Grumbling, but because she knew he was right, she moved back over to the large rock they'd used as a seat, and sat.

The mournful look on her face made him smile.

"Be careful," she said.

"I'll be back as soon as I know it's safe." He pressed a

kiss on her mouth. Then he went to the ledge and slid into the dark water.

He surfaced in the center of the pond to a sun-dappled forest.

No gunshots. Did that mean it was over or that it hadn't yet started?

Chapter 16

Moving through the forest toward the Naessan camp, Chase listened carefully. If he heard Prince Kerwin's dogs, he'd know things hadn't gone as planned.

When he reached the trail that led to the bunker, he saw Silvershire troops guarding the door.

He'd asked Carrington for a few paratroopers. The Silvershire Royal Air Force had delivered.

Emerging from the woods, he kept his hands up, in plain sight. They held him at gunpoint and summoned their commander, who recognized Chase and ordered him released.

"Is all secure here?"

The lieutenant nodded. "But we've been unable to locate Sydney Conner. Prince Kerwin has been taken into custody. Due to the delicate situation with Naessa, we've notified Duke Carrington himself. He is on his way here. ETA is approximately one hour."

"Great." Chase swallowed. "What about Jim Keesler? Older man, gray hair. He worked for me in the PR department. Have you seen him?"

The other man's expression turned grim. "I'm sorry, sir. He didn't make it. There was some initial resistance. We returned fire. There were three casualties, all theirs. He was one. We didn't know he was there."

"He'd switched sides." Sighing heavily, Chase wished he'd had a chance to talk to the other man once more. He still didn't understand what had happened to motivate a good man to turn bad, to sell out his friends and country for money.

"Would you like to view the body?"

"No." Chase turned to head back the way he'd come.

"Where are you going, sir?" The young officer appeared confused. "You should wait to speak with the duke."

"To fetch Miss Conner. I had to hide her until you guys showed up." Chase lifted his hand in a quick wave. "I'll be back before the duke arrives."

Sydney couldn't sit still. She paced, she roamed, she talked to herself in Chase's absence. And she prayed. If she lost him…

Blinking, she swallowed to try and dispel the hot ache at the back of her throat. Chase would be fine. Any moment now, he'd emerge from the depths of the pond.

A splash, and he erupted from the water, gasping for air. Delighted, she ran to the edge and helped him pull himself up. Then, before he could catch his breath, she kissed him on the mouth. Running her fingers over his face, his arms, his hair, she couldn't seem to stop touching him.

"Hey." He grabbed her hands. "It's all right."

"You're safe." Knowing her heart was in her eyes, she met his gaze and then kissed him again.

When they drew apart, he shook his head. "Yes, I'm safe." Smiling tenderly, he touched his mouth to the tip of her nose. "And if you don't stop that, we'll never get out of here."

"It's safe?"

He nodded. "After I catch my breath, we'll go. My boss—the duke—is on his way here."

"Prince Kerwin?"

"Your father has been arrested."

She searched his face. "What about Jim?"

His smile faded. "Jim's dead. He didn't make it." Eyes dark, he held out his hand. "Come on. Let's get out of this place."

A half hour later, Sydney watched nervously as a chopper landed on the beach. A handsome man wearing a black Prada suit headed toward them. He moved with a loose-limbed, elegant sort of grace.

Sydney recognized him from television. She stiffened. "The Duke of Carrington," she whispered, wondering if he still thought she'd killed Reginald.

Putting his arm around her shoulders, Chase drew her close. He kissed her cheek. "No more worries."

"Easier said than done," she muttered, studying the man as he approached.

The duke's coffee-colored eyes were sharp as he took in the way Chase stood protectively close to Sydney.

Flashing Sydney a quick smile, he clapped Chase on the back. "When you took off, I thought you'd lost your mind. But loving my Amelia has shown me what love can make you do. She pointed out how important you are to the public relations department and that I shouldn't be too harsh on you. I've decided to take her advice."

Listening, Sydney didn't know what to say. Shortly after telling Sydney they were over, Reginald had announced his engagement to the very same Princess Amelia. Now, after a whirlwind courtship, Carrington had married her.

"Now that Reginald's dead…" Her eyes widened. "I apologize. I didn't mean to say that out loud."

"No apology necessary." The duke didn't seem offended, and Sydney let out the breath she'd been holding. "You're absolutely correct. The press has been having a field day."

Chase winced. "This was why you wanted me back in Silverton, wasn't it?"

Carrington nodded. "But you had something more important to do. I'm glad to know I can still count on you."

Filling him in on Prince Kerwin's plot, Chase kept his arm around Sydney. She tried not to keep looking for a glimpse of her sire, but couldn't seem to help herself.

"It was an added bonus that looking for Sydney uncovered the plot against Silvershire." The duke fixed Sydney with an intense look from his warm brown eyes. "I'm sorry about your father."

She started to reply automatically, "He wasn't my—" Closing her mouth, she dipped her chin in a nod. "Me too," she said instead.

The duke held out his hand. "Russell Carrington."

Stepping forward, she took it. "Pleased to meet you."

"I'm glad to finally meet you, Princess Sydney. I've heard you play and must say I thoroughly enjoyed it."

She looked at Chase. With a small shake of his head, he told her not to argue about the title.

"I've been in touch with your country. King Charles has denied any knowledge. Naessa's official line is that Prince Kerwin acted alone."

"He mentioned a few other countries." She named them.

"Thank you." He signaled to the lieutenant, who snapped to attention. "Check that out immediately."

"Yes, sir."

Carrington turned his attention back to Chase. "I have more good news for you. You two can let go of this pretend engagement of yours. Miss Conner is no longer a suspect."

Pretend engagement. Hearing the words, Sydney wondered when she'd started to forget the engagement wasn't real. The shell-shocked look on Chase's face told her he was thinking the same thing.

"Evidence has surfaced proving Sydney wasn't behind the blackmail threats or the murder. We're looking at other suspects now, chiefly a terrorist group which might be linked to Sheik Kadir Al-Nuri."

Seeming to refocus, Chase groaned. "He's coming in a month for the Founders' Day gala, isn't he?"

"Yes. And we must follow standard diplomatic procedure and assign him an aide during his visit. I'm thinking Cassandra Klein."

"Why Cassandra? Kadir's a worse playboy than Reginald was."

Carrington shrugged. "She speaks Arabic."

"Any other suspects?"

"Nikolas Donovan has requested a meeting with me."

Clearly shocked, Chase narrowed his eyes. "Why?"

"He says he wants to discuss the future of Silvershire."

"Sounds like a threat."

"Could be. Amelia doesn't think so, and I trust her judgment. But rumors are starting to circulate that Reginald's death has made Silvershire vulnerable to our enemies." The duke waved his hand toward the bunker. "Which is what must have inspired Prince Kerwin to do what he did."

"Will he stand trial?"

"I don't know. Naessa has requested custody."

"Excuse me." Sydney cleared her throat loudly. "I know you two have forgotten I exist, but this is really important to me. I'd like to make sure I heard you correctly. You said that I'm no longer a suspect in Reginald's murder, yes?" Holding her head up proudly, she eyed the duke.

He grinned. "Well done, princess. I like the way you face me, nobility to nobility." He winked at Chase. "You know, maybe you should consider making this engagement real. Sydney has a hell of a lot more class than most of the true-blue royals I know."

"I—" Chase looked trapped. He pushed a strand of his long blond hair away from his face and blew out his breath in a puff.

Sydney wanted to curl up and die.

Carrington's smile faded. "I understand. You two need to talk about what's happened, right? I'll quit meddling." With a sigh, he shook his head. "Being in love so deeply makes me look for such happiness for everyone else. Again, I apologize."

Expression now a stony mask, Chase wore his impersonal, private face. "Sydney and I have a lot to talk about. I've got some explaining to do, I think."

Her heart shattered. Just like that, she knew. Now that his assignment was clearly over, Chase clearly regretted everything.

Just like Reginald had.

Except Reginald had been a mere infatuation. She knew that now. She also knew that what she felt for Chase was the real thing.

And he, like the prince before him, like her mother and the man who'd never been her father, was going to reject her love.

She didn't think she could bear it again.

One thing she did know for certain, she wouldn't run after him as she had Reginald. Wouldn't beg him to stay. She had no reason to, apart from her love. After all, she didn't carry his child.

Her precious unborn child.

She and her baby would have each other. She'd be fine. Happy, even. Eventually.

Directing her attention to the duke, she forced a nonchalant smile. "Now that I'm no longer a suspect or in danger, I assume I'm free to go back to Naessa?"

"Correct."

"How soon?" She refused even to glance at Chase again.

Chase answered, still in PR mode. "We'll need to have a press conference and clear things up. Plus—"

"No." Interrupting him, Sydney kept her gaze on the duke, who looked puzzled. "No press conference for me. You people do what you need to do on your end to handle it. Just get me home as quickly as possible."

"Sydney—"

She made herself look at him, doing her best to hide any emotion. The wind lifted his hair to caress his square jawline and his hazel eyes looked puzzled.

He was so damn beautiful that looking at him now hurt.

"That's all right, Chase. I understand." Proud of her steady voice, she tried for a smile. It felt more like a grimace. "You're good at your job, especially the body-guard part of it. Thanks for keeping me safe."

"We still need to talk," he said. "To figure out…"

"To figure out what?"

The duke interrupted. "Can you two do this at another time? Chase, you've got to get back to work. We've got reporters here, as well as the makings of an international crisis."

The not-so-subtle reminder should serve to refocus Chase on what was important to him. He'd almost lost his job for her once. She knew he wouldn't do so again. He'd told her he lived only for his job. She was no longer his concern.

After all, she was safe now.

Turning to Carrington, she looked him up and down, as though she really was a princess, outranking him. "You're a duke, therefore you can accomplish whatever you want, no matter how much it inconveniences others. Send me home."

Glancing from her set face to Chase's, the duke looked thoughtful. "I suppose I can send you in the chopper."

"Good. Notify me when it's ready." Back straight, she walked away, making herself a solemn vow. Chase would never know he'd broken her heart, even if it killed her.

Screw his job. Sydney wouldn't even look at him. Chase started to go after her, but the duke's grip on his shoulder stopped him.

"You need to come with me. We've got a press conference to hold."

About to snarl at his boss, Chase took a deep breath.

"Chase?" Carrington watched him closely. "You've got to start working on what to say to the reporters. Spin's your specialty, and God knows we can use that now. It's not every day a crown prince from another country gets charged with a crime."

Spin? Chase shook his head. "Are the reporters here on the island?"

"Yes." Mouth quirking in a smile, the duke watched him. "They're down in the bunker, waiting. I allowed two—*The Quiz* and the *Daily Press*—to come along."

Chase's heart sank. "I'm sorry, but you'll have to go it alone. I'll understand if you no longer wish to employ me."

Still watching him closely, the duke inclined his head. "I want to make certain you understand what is important here."

"My job?" Chase let his tone show his disbelief. "I'm sorry, but—"

"No, your woman." The smile became an all-out grin.

"I want our engagement to become real." Chase dragged a hand through his hair.

"Have you asked her?"

"Well, no. But—"

"Do you love her?"

Chase swallowed. "I can't live without her."

"I see. But do you love her?"

"Yes," Chase snarled. Then, softening his tone, he started forward. "I've got to go after her. I'm sorry about the press."

"I can handle them." Carrington waved him away. "Go after her, man. I'll finish up here without you."

Chase searched the camp, and the beach. She wasn't there. One of the soldiers had seen her walk into the woods, toward the pond. But when Chase got there, he couldn't find her.

He came out of the woods on the other side of the island,

near the old shelter he'd constructed from pieces of the broken aircraft.

Back to him, Sydney stood facing the water, her hair gleaming in the sun like a newly minted penny.

She took his breath away.

As he started toward her, he rehearsed what he wanted to say for the tenth time. After all, the Wizard of PR still had a trick or two up his sleeve.

She turned to face him, sapphire eyes searching his face, and all his carefully rehearsed words flew from his head.

"Sydney." He reached for her, crushing her to him

Pushing him away, she stepped back. "What are you doing here? Oh, I nearly forgot. You said you have some explaining to do. So let's hear it."

"I wanted to explain about our engagement."

She shook her head. "No need. I understand it's not real."

Though her tone was indifferent and she tried to keep her face expressionless, he caught a glimpse of pain in her eyes.

Did she truly think he didn't love her? How was that possible?

His breath caught in his throat. "Sydney, you know how I feel."

She folded her arms across her chest. "Do I?"

"Have I not shown you?"

When she still looked doubtful, he began to speak. Not the words he'd so carefully prepared and rehearsed, but straight from his heart. "Do you remember the first time we kissed, right here?"

She gave a hesitant nod.

"I'll never forget it. You pressed a kiss against my throat, and I was lost. The first time I held you in my arms? I thought I'd drown in the storm of your eyes, I—"

She held up her hand. "Stop. You don't have to do this. I totally understand. You'll go on with your job, your life, and I'll go on with mine." She touched her stomach without hesitation. "In case you've forgotten, I'm expecting another man's baby."

He shook his head. "My baby. Ours."

Her eyes filled with tears. "What are you saying?"

"I want us to be a family. I want to raise your baby with you, as my own, and to be the only father that child will ever know." Blinking back tears of his own, he cleared his throat. "I want our engagement to be real."

Her lush mouth curved in the beginnings of a smile. "But Chase, you've never asked me."

He dropped to one knee, right there in front of their old shelter, with the ocean crashing on the rocks behind him, and the cloudless May sky as his witness.

As he opened his mouth to speak, a reporter stepped from the shadows of the trees, camera snapping.

Paul Seacrist from *The Quiz* gave them the thumbs-up sign. "Got it," he said. "Would you care to make a comment?"

Growling a warning, Chase shook his head. "Go away."

Sydney laughed. "No comment."

"Please." Chase's voice was somewhere between a snarl and a plea.

The reporter looked from him to her. Something he saw in Chase's face softened his eager expression and he nodded. "Let me give you two a little privacy."

He backed off, until he stood a comfortable distance down the beach.

"How about that?" Brows raised, Sydney looked at Chase. "Now, you were saying?"

Carefully, reverently, he took her hand. "Sydney Conner, I love you. You are all that matters to me. Will you do me the honor of truly becoming my wife?"

She smiled. "Of course, I'll marry you, Chase. How could you ever doubt it? You're my heart, my life, my everything."

With a joyous whoop, he took her in his arms. They shared a long, lingering kiss to seal the bargain. Neither paid any heed to the photographer's frantic snapping.

The following day, the picture made the front page of *The Quiz*.

* * * * *

Turn the page for a first look at
THE SHEIK AND I
by Linda Winstead Jones,
the third thrilling installment in
CAPTURING THE CROWN.
Available in June 2006.

Sheik Kadir Al-Nuri stood on the balcony of his villa on the sea, and watched the waves come in as the morning sun glinted on the gentle surf. From this vantage point he could usually see his yacht anchored in the near distance, but it had been gone for several days now. His crew was sailing the ship to the coast of Silvershire. Having his own familiar space available during his weeks there would make the long stay more tolerable, he was certain.

A private jet waited at a nearby airstrip, ready to carry Kadir and his retinue of bodyguards and aides to Silvershire. There he would not only attend the Founder's Day Gala to which he'd been invited; he would also meet with Lord Carrington, the apparent king-in-waiting. The old king was very ill, and his only son, Prince Reginald, had died under mysterious circumstances some months back. There were, of course, many suppositions about who had killed the obnoxious prince, and why, but Kadir paid little attention to rumor.

In truth, Kadir didn't care who ruled Silvershire. He desired an alliance with the ruler of that country—whoever he might be—in order to strengthen Kahani. Every affiliation he formed or strengthened, every handshake, every smile, every friendship brought Kahani another step into the modern world. Kadir wanted, more than anything, to see the country he loved move into the twenty-first century with dignity and strength.

There were those in Kahani who wanted to turn back the clock a thousand years. Most citizens wanted nothing more than peace and prosperity. A home. Food for their loved ones. Safety for their family. But for some, that was not enough. For some, life was one battle after another, and they did not want that peace. A tightness grew in Kadir's chest. Dissidence in Kahani was not new. Zahid Bin-Asfour had been a thorn in his side for a very long time. Fifteen years and four months, to be exact.

Every alliance cemented Kahani's place in the new world, but there was another reason Kadir desired a meeting with Lord Carrington. Reliable intelligence indicated that Zahid and Prince Reginald had met not long before the prince's death. Three days before, to be exact. Kadir didn't know why Zahid and the late prince had met. If Carrington had intelligence he did not…a sharing of information might be useful to both parties, and both countries.

Kadir watched a familiar figure approach from the east, the sun at the old man's back. Mukhtar ran a local market, and delivered fresh fruits and vegetables several times a week. He carried a canvas bag that bulged with lemons, grapes and almonds, Kadir's favorites, and whatever vegetables had looked best that morning. The bodyguards who surrounded the villa at all times were accustomed to the friendly vendor. As Mukhtar drew closer, Kadir could see that he did not wear his usual smile. He was not only in an uncustomary bad mood, but had apparently forgotten that Kadir was leaving the country today and would not return for several weeks, and therefore had no need for this morning's delivery. Something must have distracted the usually pleasant man.

"Good morning," Kadir called as the man approached the balcony. Mukhtar's feet dug holes into the sand, and he kept his head bowed.

Before he reached the balcony, Mukhtar stopped. He did not raise his head.

"Is everything all right?" Kadir rushed down the steps to join the old man on the sand. "You're looking rather pale. If you need a doctor…"

Mukhtar lifted his head. There were tears in his eyes. "I'm very sorry," he croaked. "I didn't have any choice, you must understand. They have my children. My daughters and my son. My new grandson." He shivered visibly. "I must do as they say. Forgive me."

The canvas bag Mukhtar carried bulged in such a way that Kadir knew—too late—that it did not contain the usual fruits and vegetables. Mukhtar's distressed face and the cleverly disguised handcuffs that Kadir had not seen until it was too late told him what was in that bag.

Kadir wondered, as he took a step closer to the old man, if the explosive apparatus would be triggered by a timer, a remote device, or the frightened vendor himself. "Let me help you. The king's guard can rescue your family. Whoever has done this, you can be sure that he has no honor. A man who would kidnap innocents to force you to this will not release his captives, no matter what you do."

Mukhtar took a step back. "He told me you would say that. He also said I should remind you that you could not save *her.*"

Kadir took a deep breath. *Zahid.* In the past few years, Bin-Asfour had spent most of his time in neighboring countries. Was he back in Kahani? Was he watching? What had precipitated this newest and boldest attempt on Kadir's life? Whatever the reason, now was not the time to allow his old enemy to taunt him into making a foolish decision. "That is the past. All that matters is now. All that matters is saving your family. I can have an explosives expert here in moments. We'll disarm the bomb, free you and set about rescuing your family. You can help me end the tyranny of a madman who wants to drag us all into the past. You can be a hero."

Mukhtar lifted his chin, and Kadir could see that his decision had been made. "Don't come any closer." He took a small step back, and then another. "I did not know what to do, Excellency. Forgive me. I am a foolish old man."

"No, you're…"

Kadir got no further before the man turned and ran. Not toward him, as was surely Zahid's intention, but away— toward the sea. The guards saw what was happening and moved forward, guns drawn.

"Don't shoot!" Kadir called. There was no need. At the moment Mukhtar was a threat only to himself. When he reached the edge of the water Mukhtar turned, and in that instant his eyes met Kadir's. The old man no longer cried. Instead, he was stalwart and determined. One hand moved toward the bag that was handcuffed to the vendor.

"No," Kadir whispered.

A powerful explosion rocked the peaceful morning, and those guards who were closest to the bomber were thrown backwards and to the ground. None were close enough to be injured—though Sayyid appeared to be stunned by the jolting fall. The sound of the blast rang in Kadir's ears, and a cloud of sand danced where the old man had once stood. Sayyid and the others who had run to stop Mukhtar from his foolishness shook off their surprise and slowly regained their footing in the sand.

Kadir turned his back to the violence and climbed the steps to the balcony. Household servants and political aides who had been preparing for the upcoming trip ran onto the balcony and were met with horror.

Kadir did not look back, as he had no desire to see what was left of a decent man on the beach. He caught his personal secretary's eyes and issued a command. "Get Sharif Al-Asad on the telephone." Sharif was a highly placed officer with the Ministry of Defense. He and Kadir had once worked together, but years ago their careers had taken very diverse paths. Still, they had managed to remain friends. Their methods of operation were different, but their ultimate goals were much the same.

Hakim nodded curtly, snapping, "Yes, Excellency," before returning to the house to do as he was told.

The others remained on the balcony, watching the scene on the beach in horror and surprise. There should be no surprise at unexpected violence, but horror…yes. An old man blowing himself up in a vain attempt to save his family was the height of horror.

Kadir had sacrificed much in the name of what was best for Kahani. He was thirty-six years old and had no wife, no children. There had been a steady succession of women in his life, all of them fun for a while but in the end…uninspiring. He could easily arrange a marriage with a suitable woman he had never met, but that would mean calling upon the ways of the past. Ways he was determined to change.

His parents were gone, and his brothers had lives and families of their own. And of late, Kadir was not always certain what he most wanted. One thing was certain: he wanted Zahid Bin-Asfour destroyed. He would not rest easy until that was done.

Hakim had Sharif on the line within minutes, and Kadir shared all the information he could, as he set the rescue of Mukhtar's family into motion. There had been a time when he would have been one of the men storming the terrorist camp in order to rescue the innocent, but these days his role in defeating terrorism took a different slant.

When Kahani was properly and securely aligned with a number of powerful nations who would come to their aid when the need arose, Zahid and those who followed him would be reduced to nothingness. These days Kadir did his best to defeat his enemies in a different way—with a smile, and a handshake, and the sincere promise of alliance.

Zahid Bin-Asfour could not fight the entire world, and Kadir intended to bring that world down on his head.

Cassandra Klein paced in the shade of a hangar. Al-Nuri's plane was scheduled to land at this small, private airport in less than fifteen minutes.

This new wrinkle was alarming, but she felt up to the task. If she wanted to rise in the ranks, she could not allow any twist or turn to alarm or distress her. If she became the aide who was able to handle any situation—even this one—she would soon be indispensable.

More than anything, Cassandra wanted to be indispensable.

His Excellency, Sheik Kadir, had requested a meeting with Lord Carrington, to take place as soon as possible. Lord Carrington was not yet ready to meet with the sheik, for a variety of reasons. Just as she had been about to leave for the airport, Cassandra had been asked by her superior, Ms. Nola Dunn, to keep the man entertained—no, *distracted* was a better word—until such time as the meeting was desirable for both parties.

Cassandra didn't know precisely why Lord Carrington didn't want to meet with his visitor from Kahani just yet, but she did know that something important was going on in the palace. Something to which a woman of her station would not be privy. There was an electricity among those in the know, an unnatural energy that kept them all on edge. Even Ms. Dunn had been edgy.

It didn't matter. One day she would be privy to everything. One day.

Cassandra knew this assignment could make or break her career in foreign service. For years, she'd studied other cultures and languages in hopes that one day she would be Silvershire's representative around the world, in places where the small country she called home had never held a position of importance. For now she was a low-level diplomatic aide, but one day—one day she would see the world.

She had done her best to make herself valuable in her present station, hoping to be noticed and promoted. During the latest computer upgrade, she'd stayed late almost every day, making sure everyone's station was in proper working order, if they asked her to help. They often did, since she was quite good with computers, and always available to assist. When Ms. Dunn's latest disaster of a secretary had made a mess of her files, Cassandra had volunteered to work on the weekends until order was restored. She was very good at restoring order.

Keeping up with news from around the world was quite important, and was a big part of her job. She had bulging files on all the countries that would be represented at the Gala, and she'd shared what she'd gathered with the others in the office. Still, none of the assignments she'd taken on to this point were as important as this one.

She recognized the sheik's jet as it landed and taxied toward the hangar. The flag of Kahani was proudly painted on the side of the jet. The time of the sheik's arrival had been a carefully guarded secret, so there was no fanfare, and no curious onlookers clamored for a peek at the entourage. There was just her and a driver who waited in the parking lot on the other side of the hangar. Cassandra straightened her spine and took a deep breath of air. Not only did she have to assist the foreign minister from Kahani with a fine balance of respect for his customs as well as respect for her own, now she had to stall him in his quest for a meeting with the duke. Too bad Lexie had already left the country. She was an expert at keeping men of all types diverted. Cassandra had never been good at diversion. She was much better suited to directness...often to the point of bluntness. Why be subtle when directly spoken words were so much more, well, direct?

The jet came to an easy halt on the runway. After a short pause, the door opened, and a stair was lowered. For a moment no one descended. Cassandra's nerves were none the better for the delay. She'd just as soon get this difficult assignment underway.

A tall, thin man in a severe dark suit was first down the stairs. He studied the area as he descended, one hand held ready over his right hip, where a weapon no doubt was housed in a holster of some type. At a crisp word from the tall man, two others descended the stairway—more quickly and not quite as openly aware. Cassandra stepped toward the jet, and immediately had the attention of all three men. She could see that they instantly assessed her as non-threatening, but they were prepared for anything. No one answered her smile.

"Good afternoon," she said, speaking in perfectly accented Arabic. "I'm Cassandra Klein, and I will be His Excellency's guide during his stay in Silvershire." She received no response from the men, none of whom was the sheik she had been sent here to meet. Was it possible that he had canceled his appearance and one of these men was his replacement? No, these men were muscle. Bodyguards, no doubt. Kahani wasn't the hotbed of terrorism some of the neighboring countries had become, but neither was it an entirely safe place. Leaders who worked to bring about change were often endangered, and she imagined Al-Nuri was no exception to that rule.

She heard a soft, deep voice from just inside the jet, and a moment later a man she recognized as Sheik Kadir appeared at the top of the stairs. Another guard was positioned behind him, and she caught a glimpse of two others—not muscle, from what little she saw of them. They were administrative assistants, no doubt. From the top of the stairs, the sheik looked down at her and smiled. Cassandra's stomach did an unexpected flip. Her heart fluttered. Oh, dear, the man's photo did not do him justice, not at all. Her smile remained in place, a wooden mask as she gathered her wits about her. Her stomach only flipped because she'd eaten that salad dressing at lunch. It had tasted good enough, but obviously it had gone bad. She steeled her heart against another flutter as the man she had been sent here to meet descended the stairs with the grace of an athlete and the smile of a movie star. Like the others, he was dressed in an expensive suit that fitted him perfectly. Unlike the others, he continued to smile.

"What a pleasure to be greeted by such beauty."

Cassandra hated it when someone, *anyone,* commented on her physical appearance when whether she was pretty had nothing to do with diplomatic service. But of course, she could say nothing to reprimand the sheik.

Oh, my, those eyes. In a moment of utter insanity her innards began to react again, and an unexpected and unwanted thought flitted through her mind.

He's the one.

No, Cassandra insisted to herself as she pushed her surprising reaction aside. Aside and down with a vengeance, until it was buried deep. The dance of her stomach, the knot in her chest, it was surely nothing more than the ill effects of bad salad dressing. She couldn't allow it to be anything else.

* * * * *

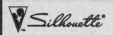

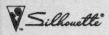

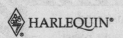
HARLEQUIN®

American ROMANCE®

IS THRILLED TO BRING YOU A
HEARTWARMING MINISERIES BY
BESTSELLING AUTHOR

Judy Christenberry

Children of TEXAS

Separated during childhood, five siblings from the
Lone Star state are destined to rediscover one another,
find true love and a build a Texas-sized family legacy
they can call their own....

You won't want to miss the fifth and
final installment of this beloved family saga!

VANESSA'S MATCH
On sale June 2006 (HAR#1117)

Also look for:

REBECCA'S LITTLE SECRET
On sale September 2004 (HAR#1033)

RACHEL'S COWBOY
On sale March 2005 (HAR#1058)

A SOLDIER'S RETURN
On sale July 2005 (HAR#1073)

A TEXAS FAMILY REUNION
On sale January 2006 (HAR #1097)

If you enjoyed what you just read,
then we've got an offer you can't resist!

Take 2 bestselling
love stories FREE!

Plus get a FREE surprise gift!

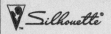

HOTEL MARCHAND

**Four sisters.
A family legacy.
And someone is out to destroy it.**

A captivating new limited continuity, launching June 2006

The most beautiful hotel in New Orleans,
and someone is out to destroy it. But mystery,
danger and some surprising family revelations
and discoveries won't stop the Marchand sisters
from protecting their birthright...
and finding love along the way.

**Hidden in the secrets of antiquity,
lies the unimagined truth...**

Introducing

a brand-new line filled with mystery
and suspense, action and adventure,
and a fascinating look into history.

And it all begins with DESTINY.

In a sealed crypt in
France, where the
terrifying legend of
the beast of Gevaudan
begins to unravel,
Annja Creed discovers
a stunning artifact
that will seal her destiny.

*Available every other
month starting
July 2006, wherever
you buy books.*

GOLD
EAGLE ®

GRA1